The
Road to
Tamazunchale

Bilingual Press/Editorial Bilingüe

General Editor
 Gary D. Keller

Managing Editor
 Karen S. Van Hooft

Senior Editor
 Mary M. Keller

Editorial Board
 Juan Goytisolo
 Francisco Jiménez
 Eduardo Rivera
 Mario Vargas Llosa

Editorial Consultant
 Tanya Fayen

Address:
Bilingual Review/Press
Hispanic Research Center
Arizona State University
P.O. Box 872702
Tempe, Arizona 85287-2702
(602) 965-3867

The Road to Tamazunchale

Clásicos Chicanos/Chicano Classics 3

Ron Arias

Bilingual Press/Editorial Bilingüe
TEMPE, ARIZONA

Third edition. First edition published by the West Coast Poetry
Review, Reno, Nev., 1975. Second edition published by Pajarito
Publications, Albuquerque, 1978.

ISBN: 0-916950-70-0

Library of Congress Catalog Card Number: 86-70700

PRINTED IN THE UNITED STATES OF AMERICA

Third printing, June 1997

Cover and text illustrations by José Antonio Burciaga

Cover design by Christopher J. Bidlack

Acknowledgments

This publication is made possible, in part, with public funds
from the New York State Council on the Arts and the National
Endowment for the Arts, a federal agency.

Eliud Martínez' "Introduction" (pages 9-24) incorporates some
material from his article "Ron Arias' *The Road to Tamazunchale:* A Chicano Novel of the New Reality," *Latin American
Literary Review*, 5, 10 (Spring-Summer 1977), 51-63. Used
with permission.

The postscript on page 126 is taken from *New Guide to Mexico
and Lower California* by Francis Toor. © 1954 by Crown Publishers, Inc. Used with permission.

About *Clásicos Chicanos/Chicano Classics*

The Clásicos Chicanos/Chicano Classics series is intended to ensure the accessibility over the long term of deserving works of Chicano literature and culture that have become unavailable over the years or that are in imminent danger of becoming inaccessible. Each of the republished volumes in the series carries with it a scholarly apparatus that includes an extended introduction contextualizing the work within Chicano literature and a bibliography of the existent works by and about the author. The series is designed to be a vehicle that will help in the recuperation of Raza literary history, maintain the instruments of our culture in our own hands, and permit the continued experience and enjoyment of our literature by both present and future generations of readers and scholars.

The Road to Tamazunchale, which was nominated for the National Book Award, was first published in 1975. As part of the Clásicos Chicanos/Chicano Classics series, it will now be available over the long term. This edition, which features a scholarly introduction by Eliud Martínez, a bibliography of works by and about Ron Arias by Ernestina N. Eger, and new illustrations by José Antonio Burciaga, reproduces the first edition in corrected form.

G.D.K.

Contents

Ron Arias'

"The Road to Tamazunchale":

Cultural Inheritance

and Literary Expression

Eliud Martínez

During the seventies, the contemporary Chicano novel arrived at a stage of maturity in the works of Tomás Rivera, Rodolfo Anaya, Miguel Méndez, Rolando Hinojosa, Alejandro Morales, Aristeo Brito, Ron Arias, and others. The novels of these writers continued to exhibit a fascination with and an interest in Chicano and Mexican cultural values, experiences, language, customs, and traditions, which characterized early Chicano poetry, drama, and novels. In the seventies, however, the maturity of the Chicano novel was reflected in the writers' greater competency in the handling of experimental literary forms and techniques, in their more sophisticated conception of fictional reality, and in their more expanded personal vision as creative writers.

To some extent the maturity of Chicano writers can be attributed to their growing knowledge of contemporary Mexican and Latin American literature and to the influence of *la nueva novela latinoamericana* on Chicano novels. Indeed, in the *nueva novela* there is a convergence of the most salient experimental and innovative narrative forms and techniques which characterize developments, movements, and trends in modern and contemporary literature and the arts. The connections between contemporary Chicano and Latin American literature bring Chicano writers into direct and indirect contact with novelists, playwrights, filmmakers, and artists from many parts of the world. Moreover, as Carlos Fuentes has pointed out in *La nueva novela hispanoamericana*, and as his own and the works of Rulfo, Carpentier, Cabrera Infante, Vargas Llosa, Cortázar, and García Márquez, among others, bear testimony, "Los latinoamericanos—diría ampliando un acierto de Octavio Paz—son hoy contemporáneos de todos los hombres. Y pueden . . . ser universales escribiendo con el lenguaje— and writing about the marvelous realities and cultural experiences,

9

Alejo Carpentier would add — de los hombres de Perú, Argentina . . . México,"[1] or Cuba.

Ron Arias' *The Road to Tamazunchale,* first published in 1975, exemplifies admirably how fundamentally close are the Chicano and the Latin American cultural experiences, on which our respective literatures focus, in the larger context of the whole world. In addition, *Tamazunchale,* like *la nueva novela,* illustrates the premise that our New World cultural inheritance is continuous and alive in the present. For these and other reasons, Ron Arias' slim novel brought contemporary Chicano literature into close association with our Latin American cultural inheritance and into a more close association with international literature and the arts than it had previously enjoyed. The interpretation of *Tamazunchale* which follows should bear out these assertions.

Gabriel García Márquez has emphasized the tremendous importance of the Latin American cultural inheritance and its literary expression. In his 1983 Nobel Prize acceptance speech before the Swedish Academy (the text was published in the *Boletín del Círculo de Cultura Cubana,* número 7, febrero de 1983), García Márquez commented at great length on a particular literary legacy of Latin Americans. "Los Cronistas de Indias," he states, "nos legaron . . . incontables," and he makes a long list of extraordinary things which the discoverers and explorers of the Indies reported having seen with their astonished eyes: improbable creatures, strange inhabitants, unexplainable phenomena, mysterious appearances and disappearances, astonishing places, magical rituals and customs, legendary events, fantastic beings, marvelous landscapes, and more. "Me atrevo a pensar," he says modestly, "que es esta realidad descomunal, y no sólo su expresión literaria, la que este año ha merecido la atención de la Academia Sueca de las Letras." And the Colombian author states that this overwhelming and marvelous reality leaves little for the imagination to invent:

> Una realidad que no es la del papel, sino que vive con nosotros y determina cada instante de nuestras incontables muertes cotidianas, y que sustenta un manantial de creación insaciable, pleno de desdicha y de belleza, del cual este colombiano errante y nostálgico no es más que una cifra más señalada por la suerte. Poetas, mendigos, músicos y profetas, guerreros y malandrines, todas las criaturas de aquella realidad desaforada hemos tenido que pedirle muy poco a la imaginación, porque el desafío mayor

para nosotros ha sido la insuficiencia de los recursos conven-
cionales para hacer creíble nuestra vida. Este es, amigos, el nudo
de nuestra soledad.

The marvelous dimensions of Latin American reality, chronicled in
the travel literature of the cronistas, García Márquez eloquently and
persuasively declares, palpitate in the daily lives of Latin Americans.
These dimensions of reality find superlative literary expression in such
works as *Cien años de soledad* and *Los pasos perdidos,* to cite only two works,
and are inspired by the "incontables" of the "Cronistas de Indias."[2]
One cannot help but think also of the extraordinary influence that travel
literature in general has had on such works as *Gulliver's Travels, Can-
dide,* and *The Narrative of Arthur Gordon Pym.*

Without suggesting qualitative comparisons or that Ron Arias is
of the stature of García Márquez, Carpentier, or the European and
American writers, one may yet say that it is to Arias' credit that he
too has found inspiration in the marvelous realities of South America,
where he has lived and travelled, and in the travel literature of the
New World. His personal vision as a writer is cosmopolitan, and in
the writing of *Tamazunchale* he drew on a variety of personal experiences, as is clear from his interview with Bruce-Novoa published
in *Chicano Authors.*[3] There he comments on the vivid and memorable
pleasure he felt when he first read *Cien años de soledad* and on the wonder
and fascination he experienced when he read "the European cronistas
of the exploration centuries," whose works "are all storehouses of life"
that undoubtedly "affect my own fictional work."

Rightly then, critical reviews and scholarly articles point to elements
of "magical realism" in *The Road to Tamazunchale* and identify
recognizable influences from Borges, García Márquez, Rulfo, and
others.[4] Ron Arias' novel, moreover, attests to the author's knowledge
of international literature, past and present. Arias has borrowed from
Cervantes' *Don Quijote* and from Goethe's *Faust,* and most likely from
Faulkner's short story "A Rose For Emily." *The Road to Tamazunchale*
is typically contemporary in many respects, in structure and form,
in the handling of time and characterization, in its overlapping of fantasy and reality, dream and magic, and in the logical development
of absurd premises. The novel contains elements that are cinematic
and self-reflexive, expressionistic and surrealistic; it exhibits a number
of artistic conventions, then, which characterize contemporary works
that subscribe to a modern conception of fictional reality, which Carlos

Fuentes, Robbe-Grillet and others call "the new reality."[5] The English prose style is lean and crisp, and Arias occasionally employs Chicano conversational idioms in a natural way. The central themes of the novel are death, aging, the journey of life, the nature of the afterlife, art-as-created, and the multifaceted Chicano experience, among others. The term "the new reality" subsumes "magical realism"[6] and calls to mind the art of Pirandello and Genet; Buñuel, Fellini, Bergman and Antonioni; Borges, Robbe-Grillet, Rulfo, Cortázar, Fuentes, and countless others. The new reality has its origins in Modernism. It provides the esthetics for much of what is considered Post-Modern — that is, contemporary art — including the novel, theater, film, and painting. The esthetic ideas, doctrines, and techniques of the new reality cut across schools and movements such as surrealism, expressionism, the theater of the absurd, the "new novel" (French and Spanish American), and so on.

In the novel the new reality represents a continuation and culmination of the modern novelist's preference for depicting interior reality and states of consciousness as opposed to exterior reality. Much of the action in *The Road to Tamazunchale* takes place in the imagination and dreams of Fausto, the novel's main protagonist. "Are you awake?" is a constant refrain in the novel. Fausto is about eighty years old and he knows that he is dying. In fact, as the reader learns at the very beginning of the novel, since his retirement six years earlier, Fausto has been leading what might be called a death in life.

Chapter One introduces the central theme of death and dying and describes Fausto's symbolic "change of skin," of which his niece Carmela remains unaware. "She must be blind, she didn't even notice. . . . Next time I'll give her my heart, and she'll say . . . Tío, don't play games. Put it back." This change of skin and the symbolic sound of a flute, heard only by Fausto and associated throughout the novel with the theme of death, propel the novel forward. Both symbolize the old man's determination to make his remaining days meaningful: his first impulse is to take a voyage to Cuzco, Peru.

The Road to Tamazunchale is characterized by an emphasis on play and make-believe, which underscores the fictionality of the novel. The lovable Fausto is able to journey back and forth in time: as he stumbles up the stairs to his bedroom in his Los Angeles home, he arrives in Peru, where buses, taxis, airplane terminals, concrete, train tracks, and telephone poles coexist with colonial viceroys, archbishops, and a procession of foot soldiers, harquebusiers, and lancers. Here Arias links Chicano literature with Spanish American fiction and the literature of travel on which it draws, and he links the colonial past and the present by making them coexist. The ripoff of a pack of cigarettes at the local black market leads Fausto to compose "an elegant, detailed report to the viceroy." Another example of make-believe is described in a later part of the novel. Fausto says to one of the wetbacks in the group which (he dreams?) he is smuggling into the United States: "When we get to where we're going, all of you must pretend you're dead." The seriousness of smuggling Mexican immigrants into the United States is handled playfully. And toward the end of the novel when a young priest comes to give the dying Fausto his last rites Fausto blesses him. "He's a strange man," says the perplexed priest to Carmela. "He likes to play games," is her reply. In this novel, death is the most serious game of all, and Fausto plays it with great frequency.

In one of the humorous episodes of the novel, Arias describes Fausto's encounter with two girls at a bus stop. Wearing his dead wife's pink nightgown as a cape and carrying a hoe which he believes to be a staff, Fausto boards the same bus that the girls take. Both girls are described as dark, one of them with dyed blonde hair. When the suspicious bus driver is rude to Fausto, Mario, an "apprentice wizard," a goateed teenager, intervenes and befriends Fausto. One is reminded of conversations between Don Quijote and Sancho Panza. This episode also makes a commentary on the Chicana's imitation of blonde Anglo women, without belaboring the point. As Fausto takes a seat, Mario waved and

> . . . gave him the thumbs-up sign. "Good try," he said as Fausto sat down. "But I'll tell you what's wrong."
> "What?"
> The boy slid over to Fausto's side and tugged at the cape. "This."
> "My cape?"
> "Yeah, it don't look too cool. I mean it's not the thing to wear when you're trying to score. . . . They don't dig capes no more. That went out two years ago."

An important convention in the arts of the twentieth century which emphasizes make-believe is the story within a story. This convention is followed in drama and film as well as in the novel. A work of art becomes, as in Hermann Hesse's *Steppenwolf*, a "magic theatre," a spectacle, in which the imagination is allowed complete liberation. In a

13

work of the new reality, vision and fantasy, hallucination and dream are celebrated. Everything imaginable and even the impossible are possible.

The Road to Tamazunchale contains a play within the novel that is important for an understanding of the novel's esthetics.[7] Arias' play within the novel allows him to comment upon the esthetics of his novel and to make that commentary an integral part of the work itself. All of chapter eleven is important for this reason, and it is intended in addition to prepare the reader for the impossible events depicted in chapter thirteen, the last chapter of the novel.

In chapter eleven, several possible titles and settings for the play within the novel are discussed by the characters. One of them, Tiburcio, proposes "Vida y muerte." After some discussion he also adds that "the title should have some mystery to it, maybe something about a man with a mask." The play is to be performed to entertain the heavy-hearted group of wetbacks smuggled by Fausto into Los Angeles. It takes place in an abandoned theater, and, as it turns out, the title of the play is "The Road to Tamazunchale."

This chapter contains a number of expressionistic details: to begin with, an abandoned theater. There are improvised props, such as the simulated bus; makeshift costumes; theatrical makeup; ambiguous dialogue; and a carnival or circus atmosphere — popcorn, candied apples, footlights, whistling, laughter, applause and bewilderment. Tiburcio, like the barker at the circus, announces the play. Everyone is in a playful, make-believe frame of mind.

At the end of the play illusion and reality meet and overlap. The characters exhibit a consciousness of role playing. The child who plays the role of Fausto gestures to the audience and invites them to join the actors. The play, therefore, discards the convention separating performers from audience and projects beyond the physical limitations of the stage to incorporate the spectators. Chapter eleven closes with Fausto in his own bed, asleep and dying, clapping his hands, much to the bewilderment of Carmela and Mario. Arias makes a cinematic transition at this point in the novel. He links the two chapters and establishes a subtle artistic continuity between them by shifting the scene or the situation and having Fausto clap his hands in both. This cinematic technique is called *linkage*.[8] The theatrical or make-believe nature of the play within the novel and the fictional nature of the novel itself are made apparent for the attentive reader by this overlapping of illusion (in this case, dream) and reality.

Illusion and reality also overlap in Arias' handling of some of his characters. In passing from modern to contemporary, the arts of the novel, theater, and film are characterized by a noteworthy development, the emergence of characters who are emphatically invented and fictional. One finds them in the works of Lautréamont, Pirandello, Kafka, Beckett, Ionesco, Buñuel, Rulfo, Fuentes, and many others — in novels, films, and plays. In numerous contemporary works one finds characters who are illusory, contradictory, and ambiguous.[9] When they are compared with traditional characters their complexity becomes even more pronounced.[10] Pure fictional creations, as Robbe-Grillet has pointed out in *For a New Novel*, are true in proportion to their falseness. And they are subject to the most extravagant mutations in the mind of the creator and to the whims and fancies of the characters themselves.

Some of the characters in *The Road to Tamazunchale* are fictions in the minds of other characters. Ana, for example, one of several Virgil-type guides for Fausto in the novel, appears to him in his imaginary voyage to Cuzco. She fuses ambiguously with Carmela in Fausto's mind and whether or not she is a prostitute who brings warmth once again to the loins of the aging Fausto remains unclear. The Buñuelian shepherd from Peru, Marcelino Huanca, with his flock of alpacas offers another example of character ambiguity. The music from his magical flute is a recurrent *leitmotif* throughout the novel. It keeps Fausto's imminent death present in the reader's mind, for Marcelino is a Bergmanesque messenger from the other world.

A humorous and surrealistic episode in *The Road to Tamazunchale* takes place on the Los Angeles Freeway; it is reminiscent of Buñuel:

"What's that?" Mario said, jumping up.

Fausto hurried to the sidewalk. "Vente, don't be afraid," he told Mario, then stepped off the curb into the mass of bobbing, furry heads. The shepherd, lagging behind, seemed confused by the traffic lights and horns. At the intersection leading to the freeway on-ramp the frightened alpacas blocked a row of funeral cars, headlights on. Fausto, shouting and waving his hoe, stumbled up the ramp and tried to turn the herd from disaster. Mario ran after him, catching a glimpse of the motorcycle escort racing to the head of the funeral procession.

In this episode Marcelino exists for both Fausto and Mario, but not for the policeman. In other parts of the novel Marcelino seems to exist only for Fausto and the flute music is heard only by him, as it is at the very beginning. In another part of the novel Fausto introduces Marcelino to Carmela and her boyfriend Jess. Marcelino is also a link between South American and Chicano characters.

Alive or dead, moreover, these strange and illusory characters wend in and out of the narrative, appear and vanish and reappear like Rulfo's dead and shadowy characters in *Pedro Páramo*. Fausto's dead wife Evangelina, for example, appears to Fausto in several parts of the novel, once inside the van in which he and Mario have hitched a ride, and another time in his bedroom, in a hallucination brought on by fever.

One of Kafka's great legacies to the arts of the twentieth century is the logical development of an absurd premise.[12] Kafka's *Metamorphosis* develops logically and in great realistic detail from the premise that a man can metamorphose into a giant insect. Buñuel's *Exterminating Angel* develops logically from the absurd premise that a group of aristocratic people cannot leave for several days the dining room of a mansion in which they find themselves inexplicably cloistered. Rulfo's *Pedro Páramo* develops logically from the absurd premise that the characters of the novel are all dead. They are *ánimas en pena*, condemned to a perpetual state of limbo or purgatory because they died in a state of sin. Realistic details are employed to produce fantastic and extraordinary effects.

Ron Arias combines the use of a purely fictional character with the logical development of an absurd premise in the depiction of the anonymous dead wetback, David, in chapter seven of *Tamazunchale*. This episode evokes Faulkner's short story "A Rose For Emily," the bizarre ending of which has apparently inspired Arias' depiction of David's relationship to Mrs. Rentería. The fact that while the anonymous dead wetback is discovered far from water, the cause of his death, which is never established, is attributed to drowning evokes García Márquez' short story "The Handsomest Drowned Man in the World" and an episode in *Cien años de soledad*. In the latter episode, the men of José Arcadio Buendía's expedition discover an enormous, intact Spanish galleon inexplicably far inland, four days' journey from the sea.

In *Tamazunchale*, David is the name which Mrs. Rentería, a lonely woman, finally decides upon for the dead wetback. This name, whether deliberate on Arias' part or not, is very suitable in view of the wetback's Michelangelesque beauty:

Everyone was silent. David was certainly the best looking young man they had ever seen, at least naked as he now lay. No one seemed to have the slightest shame before this perfect shape of a man; it was as if a statue had been placed among them. . . . Some of the men envied the wide chest, the angular jaw, and the hair, thick and wavy; the women for the most part gazed at the full, parted lips, the sunbaked arms, the long, strong legs and of course the dark, soft mound with its finger of life flopped over, head to the sky.

The old woman, like Emily in the Faulkner short story, takes the corpse of David as her lover. She bathes and shaves David, cuts his hair and powders his face, manicures his hands, and displays him. Everyone comes several times to shake the dead man's manicured hand and to admire his beauty, until he begins to decompose and smell. In the end David is not buried. "A body so perfect should not be buried," Fausto tells Marcelino, and so the shepherd, using ancient Inca knowledge, restores David's decomposing beauty. And David, in perfect condition, is taken to a place near a river, "where others can find him."

In this chapter magic and fantasy overlap. One is also reminded of Borges' "The Circular Ruins" and of a statement made by the narrator of "The Garden of Forking Paths." This statement offers a good commentary on the purely fictional nature of this character: "This book—says the narrator—is an indeterminate heap of contradictory drafts. I examined it once: in the third chapter the hero dies, in the fourth he is alive."[12] In Arias' novel, too, Fausto dies in chapter twelve; in chapter thirteen he is "alive" again.

In contemporary works, the purely fictional character is aware, in addition, of his existence as a character. As such, he or she consciously plays one or several fictional roles. In the play within the novel, Smaldino, a character, dresses as Smaldino; Mrs. Rentería, another character, plays the role of Mrs. Rentería; and "someone, probably Robert, Smaldino's eldest son, hobbled out from the side, a hoe in one hand and wearing a shabby pith helmet, a moth-eaten cape and baggy trousers. Black, crayon wrinkles were drawn above and below the eyes and at both sides of the mouth." Robert plays the part of Fausto.

In Arias' novel of the new reality, the intrusion of "real life" into a fictional work ruins the artistic effect: "Get him off the stage," says

17

one of the characters to another character in the play within the novel, referring to a third character. "He's ruining everything." Earlier in the novel, when Fausto and Marcelino walk into a Hollywood film in progress, as far as Fausto is concerned they are back in colonial times, in Colombia or Trinidad or Santa María. But as they walk across the set a filmmaker cries out: "Get those guys out! . . . What kind of costumes are those anyway?" And when an actress mistakes them for actors playing the role of beggars, Fausto is offended:

"Madame, do we look like beggars?"
"Well, I'm a whore."
"Madame, we are visitors."
"I also play a flower girl. I did that yesterday."
"I hoped we would get treated with respect."
"Don't get touchy. One day a beggar, another day a soldier.
And don't call me *madame*. I'm just a whore."

In a literary work that emphasizes its fictional nature, as these examples show, the intrusion of dream and fantasy into real life and the overlapping of illusion and reality are desirable and artistically sound. In many parts of *The Road to Tamazunchale*, Arias skillfully blurs the boundaries between art and reality. His characters suddenly appear, disappear, and reappear in the minds and perceptions of other characters.

In *The Road to Tamazunchale* certain names are extremely important. Whether or not the drowned wetback's name had been deliberately selected by Arias to suggest classical beauty, the name itself invites the kind of interpretation set forth. The title of the novel and of the play within the novel are also suggestive. The latter tends to multiply the novel's levels of reality. First of all, the name itself is real, as the author points out in his Postscript; Tamazunchale is a former Huastec capital and its precise location on the map is fixed. It is briefly described in Frances Toor's *New Guide to Mexico*. It is pronounced like "Thomas and Charlie." But Tamazunchale makes an extraordinary visual and psychological impact upon the reader, from whom this information is withheld until the very end of the novel; one had never heard of it until Arias' novel came along. And Arias artistically exploits that quality of the unknown which inheres in the unfamiliar name.

The title of Arias' novel has some mystery to it, as Tiburcio had wanted for the play within the novel. The title does not say "A Road" but *The Road* to Tamazunchale. Tiburcio, in his introduction of the

play, stresses that coming from or going to Tamazunchale, whether
it be known or not, is to travel the same road. There is *only one* way
to get there! Consider, secondly, the characters' discussions of the name. Tiburcio explains the reason for the title of the play:

"You see, whenever things go bad, whenever we don't like someone, whoever it is . . . we simply send them to Tamazunchale.
We've never really seen this place, but it sounds better than saying *the other*, if you know what I mean." (my emphasis)

And the person who plays the part of Carmela says to the person who
plays the part of Fausto:

"There's a boy who sits next to me in school, and he's always
using *that word*. The other day the teacher heard him, and he
had to stand in the corner for an hour. The teacher really got
mad because he even wrote it on the wall. But that's nothing,
I see it in the bathroom all the time." (my emphasis)

But the character who plays Fausto expresses a different view:

"Mijita . . . everyone should go to Tamazunchale."
"What's it like?"
"Like any other place. Oh, a few things are different . . . if
you want them to be."

In Tamazunchale, he says, she can be anything she wants to be, a
flower, the sun, the moon, the stars, a song of a million sounds, or
a little girl. She will be able to see all her friends there. When she asks
whether they are going to die, he replies that no one dies in Tamazunchale. Some people pretend to die, and others, he admits, do die and
are buried. But then "they usually see how stupid it is to die, so they
come out of the earth and do something else." In Tamazunchale there
is complete freedom to be everything and everyone, even to be nothing.

In these commentaries, taken in connection with Fausto's "voyage"
toward death, the name "Tamazunchale" acquires a serious vagueness
and a deadly strangeness. "Tamazunchale" becomes a metaphor for
the other world, to which there is only one road, only way to go—by
dying! Since no one has ever come back from there, no one knows
what it is like. The novel as a whole, its central theme of death and
dying, the strange events depicted in the last chapter, Fausto's final
arrival in Tamazunchale where the impossible is possible—all this

strongly supports the interpretation that Arias has used the name as a metaphor for the world beyond. According to the views of the characters, Tamazunchale can be hell or limbo or purgatory or paradise. It is one and all of them because the novel itself admits them all as possibilities.

For Fausto, then, life is a one way journey toward death. His journey is a quest for knowledge and beauty. The events through which Fausto passes and how he passes through them offer a commentary on death. *The Road to Tamazunchale* raises but does not answer the question concerning the state of souls after death. Where does the soul go? Is the grave the final "home" of the soul as well as of the body? At the end of this novel Fausto goes to Tamazunchale. For Fausto, Tamazunchale is Paradise. Hence, the last chapter communicates an exuberant joy and closes with a message of hope.

Tamazunchale names the afterlife without specifying its geography; it points to it symbolically. Another very important name is that of the main protagonist. "Fausto" is charged with significations. Fausto's discontent with his death in life, his aspiration to transcend earthly knowledge and physical limitations—these invoke Fausto's legendary namesake, the Faust of Goethe. In the same way, because Fausto Tejada is a dreamer and an adventurer, because he wears a "helmet" and a "cape" and carries a "staff," because he is a mockhero who fights imaginary battles, not with windmills but with shadows, Fausto reminds one, in addition, of Cervantes' knight-errant of the sorrowful countenance. Notable, too, in *The Road to Tamazunchale* is the number of guides—Ana, Carmela, Mario the apprentice-wizard, Marcelino Huanca (and Fausto himself is a guide for the wetbacks)—who lead Fausto through his imaginary and real experiences. In the end, Fausto is himself the guide in Tamazunchale.

Arias' *The Road to Tamazunchale* deals with universal themes that bring the Chicano experience into focus. The language of Arias' characters, particularly that of Mario, conveys an aspect of that experience, its linguistic reality. Arias has captured the special flavor, the rhythm and idioms of Chicano popular and conversational speech. The sprinkling of Spanish throughout the novel is always natural, never forced. There is a sense of shared cultural values among the characters. For example, Mexican superstition, folk medicine, and the Catholic religion amalgamate in the characters' attitudes toward death. Arias even gently pokes fun at the drinking that takes place at a funeral and at the attitude toward Mexico which Evangelina expresses. The atmosphere of Los Angeles, the largest Mexican city outside of Mexico, is also felt in this novel. Even the little episode describing Fausto's encounter with the two girls at the bus stop makes a significant commentary on a facet of the Chicano experience in the United States. Very significant is "the wetback problem," a theme that runs through the novel. Illegal immigration is a vital and sometimes explosive issue today. Arias also taps the Indian heritage of Chicanos and the identification with Spanish American literary and cultural values. In the case of the Indian heritage, mirrors are important in Chicano novels, as when Fausto "washed himself in the bathroom. Puro indio, he thought, looking at the hairless face in the mirror. You're more indio than a Tarahumara, his wife used to say." These and other facets of the Chicano experience are given artistic expression in the novel.

The Road to Tamazunchale, as a Chicano novel, has liberated itself from dogmas, as Tomás Rivera has said. Chicano writers, in Rivera's words, "need to represent and make concrete every angle and side of the Chicano. Our intent in literature, then, has to be totally human." Ron Arias responds successfully to that need.

In terms of craftsmanship and artistry, no Chicano novel before *The Road to Tamazunchale* had tapped the artistic resources of the modern and contemporary novel (and the arts) in a comparable way. Arias' understanding and command of new reality forms and techniques is commendable. His handling of character is deserving of praise. Other traits of the novelist are equally worthy: the skillful way he develops episodes logically from absurd premises, the imaginative use of the play within the novel, his employment of cinematic transitions, the blurring of illusion and reality in a number of unusual and ambiguous episodes, his structural handling of time, the effective depiction of numerous processions—of *alpacas,* of funeral cars, of torchlights, of foot soldiers, of actors, of wetbacks—the expressionistic rendering of certain scenes, the defamiliarization of real places, and in general the admirable compression of a wealth of detail, among others.

The Road to Tamazunchale, moreover, contains surrealistic and "nonsense" images. It includes a Borges-type inventory of books, among which are books not yet written: "an early cosmography of the known and unknown worlds," "a neglected, indexed history of historiography," and "an anthology of uninvented myths."

The Road to Tamazunchale, then, is a carefully crafted work which exhibits and places in the service of Chicano literature a large number of artistic resources. For this reason it has been a pacesetter and it marks a new direction for Chicano literature. *The Road to Tamazunchale* points toward the conviction that all literatures, all cultures, and all the arts cross-fertilize one another. This conviction, I believe, is fundamental to artistic contemporaneity. *The Road to Tamazunchale* is an international novel. It is a significant contribution to American literature by a Chicano writer.

Finally, Ron Arias' novel attests that at the mature stage of contemporary Chicano literature, with a few notable precedents, other dimensions of the Chicano are receiving literary expression. In the future, one may safely predict, the limits of Chicano literary art will be cast aside. Reclaiming more and more of the Mexican heritage and our New World inheritance, Chicano writers will add, as Arias has done, to our Chicano literary images other dimensions that will reflect more contemporary experiences and a broader knowledge of the world.

While many Chicano writers may come from the barrio, a good number of them have attended, or are now attending and teaching at American colleges and universities. Some Chicanos have never lived in barrios. Like contemporary Latin American writers, a few Chicano writers have begun to see the world beyond the barrio, have travelled within and outside of the United States, in Latin America and Europe. In the future Chicano literature will also mirror the new experiences of Chicanos and Chicanas: of being graduate students, of university life, of being professors and teachers, of travel, of being evaluated for tenure, and of a consciousness of becoming and being writers. Chicano literature will also reflect an expanding knowledge of foreign lands, cultures, languages and the arts, the creative process, and world history. Like contemporary writers in Mexico and Spanish America, Chicano authors will discover, without abandoning our multifaceted Chicano world, that the whole world and the treasures of civilization belong to everyone. As this immensely significant discovery progresses, the limits of Chicano literature will gradually disappear and our whole cultural inheritance and literary expression will take its place among those of the world.

University of California
Riverside

Notes

I am grateful to the *Latin American Literary Review* for permission to incorporate material from my article "Ron Arias' *The Road to Tamazunchale:* A Chicano Novel of the New Reality," published in Vol. V, No. 10, Spring–Summer 1977, pp. 51–63. Readers who wish the most complete and updated list of critical sources on Ron Arias and his work are invited to consult the excellent bibliography on Ron Arias by Tina Eger at the end of this volume. I am grateful to the UC Riverside Committee on Research for an intramural grant that assisted me in the writing of the present essay.

[1] Carlos Fuentes, *La nueva novela hispanoamericana* (Mexico: Joaquín Mortiz, 1969), p. 32.

[2] Alejo Carpentier, in *Tientos y diferencias* (Montevideo: Arca Ed., 1967), identifies many aspects of Latin American reality to which the *nueva novela* subsequently gave superlative literary expression.

Fernando Alegría, in "García Márquez: The Reality of Latin America" (Riverside, California: UC Riverside *Latin American Studies Commemorative Series,* No. 7, April 1984; Kemy Oyarzún and William Megenney, eds.), pp. 4–18, clearly establishes a direct connection between García Márquez' literary expression and that of the cronistas de Indias.

[3] (Austin: University of Texas Press, 1980). The interview with Ron Arias is on pp. 235–52.

[4] For a complete, updated bibliography of secondary scholarly sources, see Tina Eger, op. cit.

[5] Carlos Fuentes, op. cit. Alain Robbe-Grillet, *For a New Novel* (New York: Grove Press, 1965). Sections of Fuentes' work appeared in slightly different form in Juan Loveluck, ed., *La novela hispanoamericana* (Santiago de Chile: Ed. Universitaria, 1969), pp. 162–92. See also Vivian Mercier, *A Reader's Guide To The New Novel From Queneau to Pinget* (New York: Farrar, Straus and Giroux, 1971 ed.), espec. the Introduction, pp. 3–42, and the article by María Teresa Babín, "La antinovela en Hispanoamérica," *Revista Hispánica Moderna,* XXXIV (1968), pp. 523–32. These works discuss the esthetics of the new reality.

Cortázar's *Rayuela* (Buenos Aires: Ed. Sudamericana, 1963) [*Hopscotch* (New York: NAL Plume Books, 1966, excellently translated by Gregory Rabassa)] discusses throughout, but particularly in the third and final section beginning with chapter 57, the esthetics of the anti-novel and the new reality.

[6] See Alejo Carpentier, op. cit. Sections of this work appear in Juan Loveluck, ed., op. cit., pp. 137–61, under the title, "Problemática de la actual novela latinoamericana." The journal *Nueva Narrativa Hispanoamericana,* Vol I (enero 1971), contains two articles which deal with the new reality: Eduardo Camacho Guizado, "Notas sobre la nueva novela hispanoamericana," pp. 133–35; and Jaime Giordano, "Hacia una definición del realismo en la novela hispanoamericana contemporánea," pp. 127–32. Vol. III (septiembre 1973) contains Emil Volek's "Realismo mágico: Notas sobre su génesis y naturaleza en Alejo Carpentier," pp. 257–74.

[7] The convention—in several of the arts—of a story within a story or of a work of art that deals with the subject of the creative process has not, to my knowledge, been the subject of a book or monograph-type study as it deserves. There are, however, a few scholarly works that recognize and deal with this convention. Roger Shattuck's admirable *The Banquet Years* (New York: Anchor Books, 1961) has a chapter called "The Art of Stillness," pp. 325–52, that relates self-reflexive art to a number of significant artistic forms and preoccupations in the arts from 1885 to 1918. Elizabeth Sewell has isolated and discussed commendably this convention in her focussed study, *Paul Valéry: The Mind in The Mirror* (New Haven: Yale University Press, 1952). She has mistakenly concluded, however, that the use of this convention has lapsed after Valéry. T. S. Eliot has attributed this convention to Edgar Allen Poe and traced its transmission in modern poetry in his essay "From Poe to Valéry," *To Criticize The Critic* (New York: Noonday, 1965), pp. 27–42. We know now that Miguel de Cervantes and Lawrence Sterne preceded Poe.

[8] Gerald Mast, *A Short History of the Movies* (New York: Bobbs Merill Company, 1971), contains good, succinct discussions of linkage, pp. 207 ff., and *montage*, pp. 192–95.

[9] It is not possible to mention all the many great antecedents of these purely fictional characters in modern experimental novels, plays, and films. Symbolism, dada, surrealism, expressionism, and the modern psychological novel have all contributed immeasurably to this significant development in the arts of the twentieth century.

[10] For a comparison of traditional and modern characterization see David Daiches' *The Novel and The Modern World* (Chicago: University of Chicago Press, 1967 ed.), Chapter 2, pp. 12–24.

[11] Literary methods related to absurdity and the irrational are discussed in Michael Benedikt's Introduction to *Modern French Theatre,* edited by Benedikt and George E. Wellwarth (New York: E. P. Dutton, 1966); and by Martin Esslin, in his Introduction to *The Theatre of The Absurd* (New York: Anchor Books, 1969 revised ed.), where he distinguishes between the existentialist writers' logical development of absurd premises and their absurd development by playwrights of the Theatre of the Absurd. *Modern French Theatre* is an anthology of avant-garde, dada, and surrealist plays that exemplify several artistic methods employed by dramatists to develop absurd premises.

[12] *Labyrinths* (New York, New Directions, 1964 ed.), p. 24.

"Some wanted to turn back, but others, who must have been more courageous or curious, determined to see the mysterious place. . . . So they climbed up through the ashes and finally reached the summit in a cloud of heavy smoke."

Istoria de la Conquista de México
(by Francisco López de Gómara)

"Must I go like the flowers that die?
Won't anything be left of my name,
nothing of my life here on earth?
At least flowers . . .
at least songs. . . ."

(Nahuatl poem from
Cantos de Huezozingo)

*To Joan for patience
and to Julia for inspiration*

ONE

Fausto lifted his left arm and examined the purple splotches. Liver. Liver caused them. He tugged at the largest one, near the wrist. His fingertips raised the pouch of skin as if it were a small, wrinkled tent. He tugged harder, expecting the tissue to tear. The skin drew tight at the elbow. Slowly it began to rip, peeling from the muscle. No blood. The operation would be clean, like slipping off nylon hose. He always had trouble removing chicken skins, but this, he could see, would be easier.

It bunched at the knuckles, above the fingernails. Carefully he pulled each fingertip as he would a glove. The rest was simple, and soon his body lay gleaming under the fragile light of the table lamp. A stubborn piece of skin remained under his little toe. But what's a toe? She won't be looking at my toe.

Fausto folded his feather-light suit neatly in the meatless palm of one hand, closed his naked eyelids and waited for his niece.

"Tío, are you awake?" Carmela leaned over the bed.

"Can't you see?" Fausto opened his palm to show her the wad of skin. It fell to the floor.

"You want some more Kleenex?" she asked and pushed the tissue box closer.

Fausto moved his legs over the edge of the bed, bent down and picked up the skin. She must be blind, she didn't even notice. He unfolded the dry tissue, methodically spreading it on the bedcover, stretching the legs and arms their full length. He coughed, and the skin blew off the bed. Maybe she didn't see because it's too dark. But my face? No hair . . . all bony. Next time I'll give her my heart, and she'll say, Tío, what's this? Tío, don't play games. Put it back.

Carmela waited for her uncle to slip back under the sheet and blankets. She always expected the worst, or at least him lying on the floor blacked out from a stroke or a broken bone. Twice he was in the hospital after heart attacks. She had seen him later, straining to speak, with a tube in one arm and another up a nostril. Since then he took pills for chest pains. Smoking regularly.

"I'll leave your breakfast on the kitchen table."

"You're not staying?"

"I thought I'd do some shopping before work. All you've got in the refrigerator are those little bowls of leftovers. The barbecued veal I got you was already moldy. So was the squash."

"Mijita, can you buy me more cigarettes? The money's on the table."

"Don't be silly. Keep your money."

At the doorway Carmela turned and noticed his feverish eyes. Wide-open, they glistened in the dim light. Fausto lay still, listening to the faint groan of freeway traffic. He heard the front door slam shut and relaxed. Slowly he stood, then shuffled to the window and peered through the rusty screen, across the river to the tracks. More smog. For six years he had shuffled to the window, to the bathroom, down to the kitchen, through gloomy rooms, resting, listening to the radio, reading, turning thin, impatient, waiting for the end. Six years ago she had convinced him to stop work.

"One of these days you'll have to stop. You can't go on forever." And that night she had watched him return home in the dark, struggling up the veranda steps, one arm dragging his briefcase.

Fausto sat in the armchair, looking dreamily at his niece. He hadn't sold a book in two weeks. Not like his best days when he would wander the Eastside, from Five Points to Bell Gardens, like a man treading gold. In one afternoon he could sell three or four dictionaries, the first volume of an eighteen-volume Junior Book of Knowledge set, and at least a half a dozen cookbooks in Spanish or in English.

"Fine," Fausto said.

"Fine what?"

"No more work."

"You'll stay home?"

"I'll stay."

Now, years later, he felt as if his muscles were finally turning to worms, his lungs to leaves and his bones to petrified stone. Suddenly the monstrous dread of dying seized his mind, his brain itched, and he trembled like a naked child in the snow. No! he shouted. It can't happen, it won't happen! As long as I breathe, it won't happen . . . .

In silence the old man listened carefully for the song of life. Curled in the darkness somewhere beyond the house, it beckoned with the faint, soft sound of a flute. Then it was gone.

He would leave at once. He considered strapping on his buckler but decided it would be more of a nuisance than a help. Besides, he could barely lift the sword. What would he do with the buckler? Maybe he should leave them both. But why worry now? These were details he could take care of in Peru.

Before dressing he washed himself in the bathroom. Puro indio, he thought, looking at the hairless face in the mirror. You're more indio than a Tarahumara, his wife used to say. He wiped his face dry, wet it with cologne, then trimmed his sideburns with the cuticle scissors. The face hung in the mirror a moment longer.

He gathered his clothes in the bedroom. The drapes were open, the shade up, as Carmela had left them. Quickly he put his arms into the smoking jacket, worn to the lining at the elbows, adjusted his ascot and pulled on an uncreased pair of khaki trousers. As he hurried toward the stairs, his slippers slapped against his bare heels.

He could hardly wait. Should he send a message to the viceroy? Surely news of his coming would bolster morale of the Cuzco garrison. Cuzco, Navel of the World, the very soul of Inca greatness and power. Cuzco. Again he tasted the word and steadied himself on the banister. Perhaps he should make the climb by land instead of taking the plane. It was safer, and this way he could inspect the terrain. Yes, by land, perhaps on the bus. He was never the best of horsemen.

Excitement rose in his throat, and suddenly his fingers had sunk into the carpet. In the kitchen the mute parakeet cracked a seed and almost spoke. And from outside the house came the shrill, metallic sound of freight car wheels rolling into the yard.

Fausto rushed through Lima and headed into the mountains on the first bus out. He hardly glimpsed the city, except for the smog, or the drizzle, he wasn't certain. Now and then he saw a church, a plaza, the face of food in the window, but most of the time he slept, hoping he could endure the dusty, jarring ride into the sierra.

Arriving in Huancayo, he quickly smoked his last American cigarette. Desperate, he searched the streets, approaching vendors, entering stores, combing the open market. Nothing. Finally the black market emerged in the form of a small mestizo in a rumpled, threadbare suit. Although Fausto's Spanish wasn't the best, he noticed the man's speech was ungrammatical but to the point.

The stranger led him through a low doorway into a cavelike room. Along the whitewashed walls dark figures, mostly hunched over tables, hardly noticed him. The air reeked of stale grease and warm chicha. Fausto waited in the outdoor courtyard while the man climbed a stairway and disappeared in a room above the restaurant. The stranger returned with his sale wrapped in brown paper, received his money with a grin and left. Fausto ripped off the paper; one pack was missing. His first setback.

Before leaving Huancayo he composed an elegant, detailed report to the viceroy. Numerous violations of trade and customs regulations by well-organized native elements . . . bound to undermine authority. Then a few hints on the leader's whereabouts. Fausto made no mention of punishment; the thought of blood sickened him.

On the way to Cuzco he suffered an attack of diarrhea, almost forcing him to halt the journey. He squirmed in his seat for hours, doubling over and clenching his fists. Once he begged the driver to stop. The narrow, shoulderless road clung to the rock above a two-thousand-foot drop into the Apurímac River.

The driver refused, ordering his passenger to wait a while longer. But Fausto's patience had been drained miles back. He persisted, almost in tears. Meanwhile the other passengers craned their necks to catch the outcome of the argument.

"Stop!"

"No!"

"Stop or I'll report you to the authorities."

"Only God can stop this bus."

"And the archbishop . . .?"

The driver halted the bus and opened the door. "One minute."

"Two!"

"One . . . I'm counting."

Fausto carefully set his feet on the ground, dropped his trousers and squatted. Between his legs he could see the gleaming thread of river far below.

As he hobbled back to his seat in the middle of the bus, several passengers smiled sympathetically. He should have taken the plane.

At last they approached Cuzco, and Fausto leaned over his neighbor's armrest for a glimpse. No, it wasn't like the Valley of Mexico. Tenochtitlán was finer, somehow grander. Cuzco seemed a gray, hillside mass of stone. But below the city, along the highway, he could see the green fields, young with corn, wheat, barley and potato plants. Indian families squatted in doorways, watching the bus jog by in swirls of dust.

This time Fausto ignored the driver's refusal to stop and simply descended from the machine of noise, odors of urine and grimy bodies. After the dust settled, he breathed deeply and marched ahead. Leaving the road, he struggled to push away annoying reminders of time. Telephone poles along the train tracks refused to vanish, a billboard advertising Cuzqueña beer remained in the distance.

But Fausto was determined to enter the city grandly, mounted, leading an army of foot soldiers, arquebusiers and lancers. In a loud voice he ordered the right flank brought up to spread itself across the fields. Careful with the corn, he shouted. And don't harm anyone! It has to be a peaceful entrance.

Behind a cluster of huts several farmers clutched their children and ran into their homes. Chickens scattered and dogs curled their tails at the sound of pounding hooves.

But as the commander approached the new airport on the south side of the city, he winced. He should be on the *north* side. What did the map say . . .? He had left it on the bus. The thin air had tired him, and Fausto began to breathe harder, turning his face to the rich, cloudless sky. Dizzy, he reluctantly ordered the army to continue without him.

Then he crossed the concrete runway, slowly passed through the new terminal building and called for a taxi. A good hotel, he told the driver. A clean one.

After his nap, Fausto relaxed between the starched sheets. He admired the strong, wooden ceiling beams, the burnished tile floor, the massive, iron-hinged door. Leaving his bed, he touched the smooth, white walls, the dark, hand-carved crucifix. Months of labor, of fine Iberian skill. His reverie took him to the balcony where he flung open the latticed shutters. Below him in the empty plaza a dreamy-eyed llama glanced at the odd figure in pajamas.

Later two Indian boys helped him bathe. Then they trimmed his hair, fingernails and toenails. Finally they dressed him. The silky swish of his lace cuffs reminded him of Carmela's best mantilla. It seemed nothing had been spared the viceroy's hospitality. Perfumed and powdered, Fausto left for the noon meal. He asked for two poached eggs, a dish of cottage cheese, a veal steak and three choices of ice cream.

"And waiter," Fausto added, "tell his excellency I'm most grateful for his attention."

"The best is yet to come," the young man said with a wink.

"What's that?"

"I can't tell you . . . . You'll see."

During the meal Fausto's anxiety grew. What would happen to him? Was he being fattened like a hog before slaughter? Worse, how could he explain his mission to the viceroy if he himself didn't know? A man at arms? Fausto laughed nervously and pushed away the steak. He had no army, no weapons. Who would believe him? On the other hand . . . he might be a pilgrim . . . But where was he going? What shrine? Maybe a courtier? A merchant? An emissary from Panama? No, none of these would do. But the truth was even flimsier.

Fausto abruptly left the table and hurried toward the elevator. He was afraid this might happen. A man just doesn't wander about without a purpose.

In his room Carmela was waiting for him. At first her beauty left him speechless. She sat on the edge of the bed with her back to the afternoon light, her long black hair spread over her shoulders.

"Mijita," Fausto stammered, "what are you doing here? I thought you were at work."

"I am. I was told to come."

"I don't understand . . . . You don't work here."

"Listen, let's get started. It's much more fun than talking. Or have you forgotten how?"

Fausto blushed. "Carmela!"

"My name's not Carmela. It's Ana."

"But you're my niece."

"I never saw you before. But I suppose I could be Carmela . . . for a while."

Fausto palmed his thinning hair and shook his head.

"You don't want to do this, do you?" Ana said flatly.

"I don't think so, I've got a headache."

"I'll take it away, let me try."

"No, I'm tired."

Ana kicked off her sandals, unbuttoned her blouse and began to pull her arms out the sleeves.

"I just want to lie down," Fausto said as her skirt dropped to the floor. "If you want, you can rub my temples."

"Alright, old man, lie down. I'll rub your temples."

She placed his head between her legs, looked at the ceiling and sighed. Under the steady pressure of her hands, Fausto soon fell asleep.

When he woke, Ana was sitting next to him on the wooden seat of a train. Fausto squinted at the sudden light. Through the window he could see a herd of dairy cows in the shade of a lone eucalyptus tree.

"What's this?" he asked.

"A train."

"I mean where am I? Where are we going?"

"You don't belong in Cuzco, I could see that. You even said so in your sleep. The trip shouldn't take too long, and I think you'll like it."

"Is this the viceroy's idea?"

"No, it's mine. I'm taking you where few men have ever been."

"Where's that?"

"There, beyond the clouds."

In the distance above a few scattered clouds, Fausto could see the giant white peak. He turned to Ana, and she patted his hand as if to ease his fear. She wore many skirts, a rough cotton blouse, and the tire soles of her sandals were worn and curved up at the edge.

The narrow-gauge train wound its way down through the gorge of the Urubamba River. From Cuzco the trip had been a descent of some eight thousand feet, from the sparse grasses of the altiplano to the warm, humid lushness of the Amazon's edge. A matter of minutes at one point, and the little train entered the tropics. Fountains of tangled vines and broad, lustrous leaves pushed from both sides. Life strained from every rock. Passing quickly beneath Machu Picchu, Fausto gazed at the rock-hewn terraces and for a moment forgot the arthritic jabs in his limbs.

They left the train at a stop where the gorge widens to a warm plain of coca and coffee farms. Ana helped him to the ground and they started up a narrow valley to the west.

Fausto fought exhaustion most of the afternoon. The huge greenness of nature squeezed itself upon the trail, and it was all he could do to keep his legs moving. After several hours of trudging behind Ana, he began to regret leaving home. He longed for his armchair, his bed, his dinner by the kitchen radio, his books and the quiet company of his parakeet.

"Stop, Ana."

"Again?"

"A few minutes . . . . I'll be fine."

"Maybe we shouldn't have come."

"I started this, I'll finish it," Fausto said, trying to sound firm.

After a short rest, the march continued. Several times he tripped and cursed his luck. The trail seemed to vanish, and he no longer could see Ana. The jungle heat tightened around his neck and

35

chest. The air turned dark, and he glimpsed a vague, motionless figure. This was his chance. He would charge the intruder. If it were death, he would impale the monster to the hilt. But with what? Fausto asked feebly. He waved his arms weakly at the silhouette, crashed into a tree and toppled over.

Ana discovered him tangled in thick cords of vines, on his back and unable to free himself. "I thought I had lost you," she said, cutting him loose with her machete.

"I must have fainted," Fausto said, relieved at the touch of her hands.

"Not far from here is a spring. You can rest there."

They followed the trail for a short distance, then Ana skipped ahead toward the sound of water. When Fausto arrived, he saw her playfully splashing her feet between two puma heads that spouted small, clear streams into a rock-carved basin. A mild breeze blew flower petals over her glistening body.

She gestured with a nod toward the water. Fausto hesitated, then approached, and she gently removed his clothes, urged him in the snow-fed pool and massaged his back and shoulders. Afterward he slept in the shade of a mango tree on tiny ferns and tender blades of grass. She kept the insects away with a young palm branch, occasionally soothing his temples.

When he woke, she was sitting beside him, wild lucma fruit in her lap. She rubbed his knees a while longer, then brought him water to drink.

Now they would begin the steepest climb, several hours' journey to the barren uplands above the valley.

On the way they passed through a cloud-forest of weird, root-twisted shrubs and moist, darkened hollows surrounded by spongy earth. The gnarled branches of these stunted, phantom trees seemed to reach out and block the trail. Ana explained that many travelers had been trapped here and they lived on as insects, bats, even rocks.

"Don't worry," she said. "We'll be out soon."

Fausto hobbled after her and as they emerged into the fading light of nightfall, he saw the tiny huts scattered over the wide, steep slopes. Human figures, alpacas and sheep moved beneath the glacier basins.

Ana begged him to stay on his feet. "We must hurry, something has happened . . . I can feel it."

"I can't, you go on ahead."

"Please, papacito. It's not far."

"I can't . . ."

"You must!"

When the sky darkened, Ana cried out. Fausto swayed, leaned against her, and the two fell. She left him and ran to catch the long procession of torchlights winding up the mountain toward the snow.

Gasping, he clutched the knot of fire in his chest and struggled forward. Again and again he called out. Once a child, lingering behind the procession, turned and beckoned with his hand. For a long while Fausto would fall, catch his breath, then stagger on in dizzying bursts of will.

Eventually he crawled onto the hard snow, saw the group in the distance and pulled himself closer. In the moonlight the men danced on the eerie whiteness, their ponchos whirling in one great circle around the women who kneeled in the center, sending their wails to the rocky crags above.

On hands and knees Fausto moved into the circle and reached the crude platform where Ana helped him to lie down. Around them, the mourners tore the air with shouts and beat the ground. Fausto was too tired to refuse their grief. They mean well . . . but why me?

"Ana?" Fausto whispered.

"It's Carmela."

"Yes, Carmela . . . . Don't go."

"I'm right here," she said and wiped his forehead.

Far away an unknown shepherd raised his flute and released a long, melancholy note, then another, and another. Fausto smiled.

"Hear that, mijita?"

"Yes, Tío."

"It's beautiful . . . . I can't think of anything more beautiful."

THREE

"Tío, dinner's ready!"

Fausto did not answer. Carmela rapped her fingertips on the table and looked at the cottage cheese.

She climbed the stairs, called again, then entered the darkened room on tiptoes. The blankets were bunched on one side of the bed. "Tío," she whispered, "where are you?" She turned on the night table lamp and examined the bed. "Wake up," she pleaded.

Fausto lay on the far edge of the bed, his small head covered by the rumpled sheet. Carmela felt the form and pulled back the blankets. Fausto did not move. She shook his limp hand, and his eyebrow moved slightly.

"Tío, why are you playing dead?"

After a moment, Fausto opened his eyes. "I'm hungry," he said in a tired voice.

"You scared me. You weren't asleep, were you?"

"No, mijita. I thought I was dead." Fausto sat up. "It happens, you know. From one day to the next, poof! Al otro mundo."

"Well, you come down and eat in this mundo. I got everything ready." She handed him his Japanese kimono and helped him with his slippers.

"Did it snow?" Fausto asked after they were seated at the table.

Carmela laughed. "Here? In Los Angeles?"

He gouged into the melon slice with his spoon. "Yes, here."

"No, Tío, it didn't . . . But maybe tomorrow."

"I was just thinking of what to wear."

"You can't go out. It's already dark."

"I'd like to see the river . . . find a little waterfall . . . ."

"The only thing there are bums and winos. Tío, can you wait till Saturday, and we'll go to the park?"

Fausto sipped his coffee and remembered his meal in Cuzco. He hadn't even touched the ice cream.

"I promised Jess we'd go to a movie tonight, and tomorrow I've got to work late."

"Jesús again?"

"Jess, Tío. He doesn't like that name." Carmela picked up her plate and walked to the sink. She wiped the scattered birdseed from the dish-drain and placed the ragged sponge behind the faucet. Earlier her uncle had changed the newspaper in Tico-Tico's cage. Besides watering the carnations next to the veranda, feeding and changing the parakeet were his only chores.

"Then I'll tell you about Peru," Fausto said.

"I thought you were in Panama . . .? No, Tío, not tonight. Really, I've got to go."

Fausto reached past the radio and peeked between the gauzy curtains. "He's not here. Siéntate, niña. You can go when he comes."

"We're going in my car, Tío."

"You mean he doesn't take you? What kind of boy is that?"

"He's alright, he just doesn't have a car. Somebody stole it." Carmela kissed him on the cheek. "Oh, I made some jello, but let it harden a little."

"When will you be home?"

"Late, so don't wait up. You know how cold the living room gets. I'll see you in the morning."

Fausto parted the curtains again and watched his niece open the picket fence gate and hurry to the old Plymouth parked at the curb. He waited for the honk, then turned away. She had lived with him and his wife since she was a baby. Evangelina died when Carmela was nine, and Fausto had to raise the girl by himself. Now she took care of him. But how long would it last? She would marry this Jesús boy, or someone else, and leave the house.

That night Fausto listened to a few tango records, old seventy-eights with brown paper jackets and scratchy voices. For once the sadness of the music bothered him, and he replaced it with the liveliest Mariachi song in his collection. Exhausted as he was, he stood on the balls of his feet and trotted around the coffee table. Evangelina sat by the television set and watched with a worried expression. "¿Qué le hace?" Fausto explained. "I'm going to die anyway."

Raising herself from the chair, she approached her husband, a small, stooped man with a dopey smile, and forgave him with a kiss. Now go to bed, he heard her say.

Fausto climbed to the bathroom, urinated and crossed the hallway. He fell onto his bed like a drunk and slept without a dream.

In the morning after Carmela left, he began searching his room for a cape. This time he would go prepared for the cold. A doublet and woolen stockings would be nice, too, if he had the right sizes and colors. But a cape would fit anyone, cover any color.

Nothing. He looked in closets, drawers, boxes, Carmela's giant armario, the attic, the linen cabinet, everywhere, in every room. Giving up in the house, he went into the backyard and waded through the weeds beneath the chirimoya and avocado trees. In the lopsided storage shed he found his wife's hatbox, filled with moth-eaten clothes. Fausto fished past the underwear and pulled out the fragile, pink cape she used to wear on cold nights. He tied the silk tassles under his chin and left the shed. Of course, the fit was perfect, and although the cloth was wrinkled and only hung down to his ribs, there was still a bit of sheen left.

For a while Fausto postured in the sunlight next to the trash cans, then marched around the old, headless incinerator. While looking up through the muzzle of smog, he stepped on a hoe, and the handle banged his forehead. "Eva," he apologized, "I need your cape. I'll put it back when I'm done."

Taking the hoe by its rusty head, he entered the house with his staff and announced he was ready. He wasn't sure where he was going, either to the river or to the mountains. Maybe the Lincoln Heights bus.

Cape flapping, Fausto reached the bus stop on Riverside Drive and sat on the bench next to two young women wearing shorts and halter tops. They stopped chewing their gum and openly examined the odd figure with the hoe. Out of the corner of his good eye Fausto could see the slender legs, shaved up to the knees. Why wear clothes, his wife would have said.

He nodded to the women and made a clicking sound with his tongue.

"Something bothering you?" the one with dyed-blonde hair asked.

"You're very beautiful."

The women looked at each other for a moment and silently seemed to agree he was harmless. The darker of the two turned. "You always that fast?"

"I only say what I see," Fausto said confidently. He smoothed the wrinkles in his cape and leaned on the hoe.

"Okay, who's the prettiest, her or me?"

"Both of you are."

"Come on, one of us has got to be prettier."

"All women are beautiful," Fausto lied.

The blonde blew a large, blue bubble, then sucked it in.

"That's a cop-out," the other said, looking serious. "Now who's prettier, me or her?"

"She is," Fausto said.

"I knew it, I knew it! It's 'cause she's blonde, right?"

The two waited for an answer. "Well?" the darker one said. "Tell us, here comes the bus."

"Because you, my dear," Fausto said, rising from the bench,

"can't blow a bubble."

The bus pulled alongside the curb and the door folded open with a creak. Fausto stepped aside. The blonde hopped up, but the other woman held his arm. "Hey, what does that got to do with it?" He turned, blocking her way.

"Nothing."

"Then why'd you say it?"

"You gonna talk all day?" the driver called down.

"Well, why'd you say it?"

"Let's go, mister, let the lady by."

"Because I knew she would get madder if I said you were prettier."

"Oh . . . ."

"And you are."

"Goddamit! I'm closing the door. You want on or not?"

"Hey, leave the old man alone," a goateed teenager shouted from the rear seat.

"Shut up, you!"

Fausto followed the young woman up the steps and dropped two coins in the meter box.

"Watch your stuff," the driver said. "I got my eye on you."

Fausto walked toward the rear, winking to the two women and passing several others who stared at him the way they would a disease. The goatee waved and gave him the thumbs-up sign. "Good try," he said as Fausto sat down. "But I'll tell you what's wrong."

"What?"

The boy slid over to Fausto's side and tugged at the cape. "This."

"My cape?"

"Yeah, it don't look too cool. I mean it's not the thing to wear when you're trying to score."

"Score?"

"The chick, man." The boy cocked his head and pointed with his nose. "They don't dig capes no more. That went out two years ago."

Fausto inspected his know-it-all neighbor. The kid was dressed all in black. His hair, combed straight back without a part, reeked of Brilliantine, and the cuffs of his long, creased shirtsleeves were turned under one fold. Inquisitive eyes, bony, triangular face. An apprentice wizard.

"Thank you for the advice," Fausto said earnestly, "but I'll keep my cape on."

"Maybe change the color?"

"No."

The boy leaned over and with his middle finger snapped the creases of his starched trousers. For a while he seemed to lose interest and stared down the aisle. The bus grated into low gear and started up the incline that led to the bridge over the river. Fausto pulled the cord with the hoe.

"Hey, I get off here too."

Fausto refused the boy's help, explaining his staff would do.

"Man," the wizard said, "I thought you was a gardener."

The two left the bus, and Fausto walked to the bridge railing and squinted at the jumble of rocks and tumbleweeds. The boy spit over the edge and counted. He spit again, waited, then turned and clapped his hands. "I know a better place."

"Better?" Fausto said, surprised.

"Yeah, it's for one-timers only. See, if you jump here, all you do is break a leg or something."

"Who said I'm going to jump?"

"Okay, you're not gonna jump."

"And what if I was? Were you going to help me?"

"Psychology, ese, psychology. See, I'd show you this other place, and nobody'd want to jump from there."

"What's your name?"

"Mario."

"Mario qué?"

"Don't be so nosy. Just Mario."

"Alright, Mario. You can help me."

"Hey, I was only playing, ese."

"Help me look for some water. There's got to be some water down there."

"Sure . . . .You had me going for a second. But you ain't gonna find no water. It's summer, remember?"

"So there's no river?"

"That's right . . . unless you wanna call that a river."

Mario studied the dejected face. "How 'bout something to drink? That'll help you."

"I don't drink."

"Come on. Nothing strong. The liquor store's right over there."

Mario led Fausto to the end of the bridge, across the parking lot to the store. A flabby-faced man behind the counter casually looked up at the tall, skinny boy in black and his short, decrepit friend.

"Wait here," Mario said, and he sauntered over the cracked

linoleum. Fausto stood in the doorway, nervously tamping his hoe on the rubber mat. The entrance bell kept ringing.

"Tell your buddy to stop that," the fat man said. "What's he think, he's in a church or something?"

"He's sick," Mario said, frowning hard. "Give us a quart . . . ."

"Some ID first."

"For a quart of milk? Come on . . . ."

"It's in the cooler, get it yourself. And tell your friend to stop that shit. It hurts my ears."

Mario motioned Fausto off the mat and went to the cooler. Returning to the counter, he bent over the fat man's racing page and whispered that Fausto was dying. "Doctor says a few more days, and that's it. No more vida for my dad."

"Poor guy. Does he know?"

"Yeah, that's why he's acting so funny."

Fausto had stopped tamping his hoe; his cape fluttered timidly under the air-conditioning vent.

"Look at those eyes . . . the yellow skin. That's a sure sign."

"Of what?"

"Cholera."

"What's that?" the fat man said, squeezing his fingers in one hand.

"Hey, he needs his fix of milk. Doctor says that's all that keeps him alive. How much I owe you?"

"Is what he's got catchy?"

"Yeah."

"What d'you bring him in here for? You guys get out!"

"Take it easy. Let me pay you first." Mario fumbled in his shirt pocket, then searched his other pockets. "I got it somewhere . . . just a minute." As he laid the contents of his wallet on the counter, the fat man stepped back.

At that moment Fausto heard the faint, high-pitched strains of a flute. He dropped his hoe and began to shuffle in circles, uttering raspy, whistling noises.

"See what I mean?" Mario said. "Sooner than I thought."

"Take it! Go on, get him out of here before he drops."

"Thank you," Mario said, gathering up his wallet pictures. "God will pay you back."

"Get him out!"

Mario hung an arm over Fausto's shoulder, and the two walked out. In the parking lot the dance continued. "Hey, you can stop now. We got the milk." Mario opened the carton spout. "Here, have some. The vato's still watching us from the window . . . . Come on, drink some, or he's gonna be after us."

Fausto put the spout to his lips. "Too cold," he said, handing it back.

"Pretend you're drinking."

"Why?"

" 'Cause you're supposed to be sick."

"I am."

"Let's get outta here, he's comin' to the door."

They crossed the street, passed through an empty Standard station and stopped behind the telephone booth. The hard cover of the Yellow Pages dangled from a chain next to a Coke bottle with cigarette stubs floating on the bottom. Mario checked the coin-return slot with his finger, shrugged and caught up with Fausto. The old man was returning to the liquor store, still whistling and pounding his hoe.

"I can't drink this stuff," Mario said. "You want it?"

"Give it to him," Fausto said and pointed along the asphalt cracks toward the restrooms. The sleeper had curled himself against the wall, using the telephone book as a pillow. Mario walked over, knelt and picked up the brown paper bag, twisted at the top. "Empty." He tapped the grizzled head. "Hey, you, want some milk?"

The man opened one glaucous eye, peeked in the carton, shook his head and turned over in another position.

Mario pushed in the spout and sat down next to the wino. The shade felt good and he wiped a finger around the inside of his buttoned-up shirt collar. Fausto remained on his feet, listening intently. The freeway traffic seemed to have swallowed the flute.

"Where you going now?" Mario asked.

"I'm not sure."

"You know, we make a good team. I didn't think you'd do it. Man, you should've seen the pendejo's face! He was so scared we could've copped anything in the store." Mario patted the wino's sockless ankle. "We should've got something for *him.*"

"Ssssh," Fausto wheezed and turned in time to see a herd of alpacas trot around the street corner.

"What's that?" Mario said, jumping up.

Fausto hurried to the sidewalk. "Vente, don't be afraid," he told Mario, then stepped off the curb into the mass of bobbing, furry heads. The shepherd, lagging behind, seemed confused by the traffic lights and horns. At the intersection leading to the freeway on-ramp the frightened alpacas blocked a row of funeral cars, headlights on. Fausto, shouting and waving his hoe, stumbled up the ramp and tried to turn the herd from disaster. Mario ran after him, catching a glimpse of the motorcycle escort racing to the head of the funeral procession.

"Hey, ese!" Mario yelled. "Forget the sheep."

At the bottom of the ramp the bewildered shepherd shrank from the screeching tires as the officer forced his bike past the rumps of the strange, skittish animals.

Mario, milk carton tucked to his ribs, made a hopeless gesture with his free hand. The officer had left his bike and was running toward Fausto. But as he left the herd, the officer slipped on some dung. Mario lost no time. Leaping over the ice-plant alongside the pavement, he reached the motorcycle, uncapped the tank and poured in the milk. By the time he finished, the officer was stiff-arming Fausto down the ramp. The alpacas had abruptly shifted and were being led by the shepherd around the curve and onto the overpass.

"Take it easy on him," Mario shouted. "He's sick."

"He's sick alright . . . taking them sheep on the freeway."

"Alpacas," Fausto corrected, glancing at the herd trotting across the bridge.

"I don't care what they are . . . . You too, kid."

"Hey, I didn't do nothin'."

"My ass. You were helping him. Both of you, get in that car." The officer, still wiping his hands from the fall, spoke to the driver of the hearse. They argued and the driver gestured to the other cars. Finally the officer returned to the prisoners and ordered them in.

"You ain't gettin' me in no hearst," Mario said.

"Shut up."

Mario whispered in Fausto's ear. The driver and another man with "Forest Lawn" embroidered on his coat pocket had opened the rear door. The driver made a crazy-sign gesture to the next car in line and pointed to the officer.

"You first," the officer told Fausto. The giant's face was flushed pink, except for the whitish pock scars, which gave him the look of a madman. Mario helped Fausto up and pushed in the hoe next to the casket.

"What's that?" the officer asked.

"My staff."

"Let me have it."

"No."

"Goddamit!" and the officer jerked it away from Fausto. It hit the gutter with a clang. "Now you, come here." Mario backed away from the giant's arm. "I said come here!"

"No way . . . ."

The driver and his assistant nonchalantly leaned against the hearse door and watched the boy in black duck between the cars, zig-zagging to the end. A woman screamed at the sight of the revolver, the wino next to the restrooms sat up, and two boys in car-club jackets yelled, "Pig!" The officer jammed the revolver into his holster and sprinted back to his motorcycle. Blocks away, Mario waved goodbye and disappeared into the Elysian High recess crowd.

The motorcycle sputtered twice, then coasted to the end of the ramp.

"Milk," the hearse driver said, casually walking over.

"Milk?"

"Yeah, he put milk in your tank."

"You think that's funny?"

"Me? no . . . ."

"Well, tell your people we're taking a ride."

"Wait a minute! You can't use the hearse to go chasing some kid."

"No, dumb-dumb, we're taking the old man in. I'll get the kid on the radio."

"You can't. He pulled some wires."

The officer dug a fist into his hip and marched around to the rear of the hearse. "Tell everybody to get back in their cars. Excitement's over." Hopping up, he poked through the wreaths covering the casket. "Alright, where is he?"

The Forest Lawn men glanced inside. "Beats me," the driver said. "Must have run away."

"Jesus! And you guys just stood around and watched?"

"I think he went over there," the assistant said.

"No, I think he's hiding behind that tree," the driver said.

"Aw, hell," the officer muttered, "you go on without me."

"You sure? We can always call off the funeral."

"Go on . . . ."

The caravan moved by, and the giant lowered himself to the curb. Raising his eyes to the hills above the freeway, he saw the alpacas disappear into the ridge of spindly pine trees. He cleared his throat loudly, gurgled and spit on the hoe.

At Forest Lawn the gravediggers had already opened their lunch pails when the late arrival appeared. The casket was pulled out, lifted by the aluminum handrails and swung around. One of the pallbearers, smaller and older than the others, seemed to falter.

"Gentlemen," the driver said, "easy does it."

"But it's heavy. Are they always this heavy?"

"Please, gentlemen. Let's not have a disaster."

The crowd moved toward the burial hole. A carpet of paper grass had been thrown over a patch of dirt just in front of a row of fold-up chairs. The casket was placed on the platform, and when everyone was seated or standing behind the chairs, the minister began. Fortunately he was behind schedule. He read quickly, skipping over words and finishing in a mumbled monotone. Done, ashes to ashes, dust to dust.

Fausto squirmed. He was nauseous and somewhat cramped by his companion. Bracing himself on the man's cold forehead, he pushed up on the casket lid, blinked at the sudden light and sat up. He smiled weakly to his audience, then slowly climbed out and walked away.

"Oh my God!"

"Is that John?"

"Do something . . . ."

"Gentlemen, please!"

"Jesus!"

"John, is that you?"

"Oh my God!"

"Gentlemen, please, the deceased is still in the casket . . ."

"Jesus!"

"John! Come back . . . ."

FOUR

Mario tilted his face horizontal with the roof, eased his '57 Impala beside the Good Humor truck and called to Fausto.

The woman in Levis clicked her money changer and handed the old man the drumstick and a dime.

"Come on, get in," Mario yelled. The dark glasses and sheen of hair were just visible behind the steering wheel.

The woman peered at the intruder. "Your friend?"

"Yeah, he's my friend," Mario answered.

She turned, took the drumstick from the shaky hands and removed the paper. "You know him, the creep in the car?"

Fausto hesitated, and she touched his arm, waiting for the confession. "He can't make you go. You stay right here."

Mario leaned over and punched the passenger door open. "Lady, the police are after him."

"I don't believe it."

"Ask him."

Fausto avoided her eyes, then nodded. Instantly she detected a criminal twitch on one side of his mouth.

"Thank you," Fausto said politely and got in the car. The woman stepped to the open window and looked in.

"We keep our guns in the trunk," Mario explained, dropping the gears into first and pulling away.

"¿Qué pasó?" Fausto asked. He licked at the drumstick peanuts.

"What do you mean, qué pasó? They're looking for you, you're a wanted man."

Fausto was silent. He had walked five blocks from the cemetery, resting twice at bus stops. A ragged poodle, two cats and a pigeon had followed him. The smell of the dead, he concluded. But the worst part about being buried is that they close the lid. How can a man breathe? See the sky! Pues not me . . . . No, señor!

"You have any cigarettes?" Fausto asked.

"Not on me."

"Here," Fausto said, offering the drumstick. "I'm not hungry."

Mario took it and began lapping at the melted chocolate on the cone. "Hey, check the glove compartment. Maybe the vato left some in there."

Fausto found a flattened Camel with half the tobacco spilled out. He struck three matches before lighting the wrinkled tip. After a long, fierce draw, a tingle of relief descended to his knees.

The sleek Chevy left the boulevard and cruised between small stucco houses with spotty green lawns. Mario drove like a bored prince, head cocked, two fingers on the steering wheel above his crotch. "Nice, eh?"

"What?"

"The car, man, the car."

"Oh, yes, very nice."

"Not really mine. I sort of borrowed it . . . tú sabes . . . till it runs out of gas."

"You stole it?"

"I'm not gonna hurt it. I've had it almost a week and not a scratch."

"That's illegal. You know that, don't you?"

"Don't gimme no lecture. I thought we was gonna be like partners. That's why I came lookin' for you. I even got your hoe." Mario motioned to the back seat with his thumb. "I picked it up after you left."

Fausto turned, a bent column of ash hanging from his lips. The cigarette butt dropped to the seat.

"Hey, be careful! This ain't my car, remember?"

Fausto apologized and flicked the butt out the window. He asked to be let out immediately, but Mario insisted they stay together. It was the perfect cover, Mario argued. A dying old man gets everybody's attention while the kid in aisle two filches radios, tape decks, clocks, clothes, jewelry . . . anything he can fit under his jacket and in his pockets.

"Well?"

"I want to go home. If you won't let me out here, take me home."

"Shit, I thought you and me . . . ."

"Take me home."

"Okay, okay."

Fausto pointed the way, and Mario seemed to accept the loss as if he had known it all along. "That's what I get for hanging around viejos. My mother always said I had this thing for old men . . . . Maybe 'cause my dad was so old . . . . He died last year."

"That's too bad," Fausto said, watching the fur dice swing beneath the windshield mirror.

"Not for him. He could hardly wait. Said at least he wouldn't have to work no more. Yeah, the old cabrón just wanted out . . . . But that ain't gonna happen to me. No way."

"How do you know it won't?"

" 'Cause I ain't gonna work."

As they turned onto Riverside Drive and neared the Elysian Park hills, Fausto asked Mario if he would mind driving to the top.

"I thought you said you lived by the river?"

"I do, but the man playing the flute . . . ."

"You mean the vato with the sheep?"

"Alpacas. That's where he went."

"I don't know, man. Ain't that where the police academy is? I don't wanna push my luck."

"We won't go near the academy. Just take me to the park."

"Okay, but then I'm leaving."

"Nothing will happen, you'll see." Fausto remembered his neighbor's face behind the tall, chain-link fence. Tiburcio had been mistakenly corraled in an Eastside roundup of Mexican illegals and was in a terrible mood. The academy tennis courts were covered with men.

"Tell them, Fausto," Tiburcio pleaded. "They won't believe me."

"I did, but they said they had to wait for more witnesses."

"So get witnesses!"

"I can't, everybody's at work. Just wait a few more hours."

Tiburcio shook the fence like an enraged baboon.

"Cálmate," Fausto said, trying to think of some consolation. "You want them to lock you up?"

"What's this?"

"I mean in jail."

"Fausto, you sound like you're working for them. Remember, you could be here too."

The rest of that afternoon Fausto sat by the fence pretending he was inside with Tiburcio. What else could he do? His neighbor would have screamed and shaken the fence if Fausto had dared take a step away.

Mario swerved onto the narrow road that bordered the picnic grounds. "You want off here?" he asked Fausto.

"Listen. Hear that?"

"Long as it ain't no siren."

"Stop . . . . Hear it?"

"Yeah. That your friend?"

"Bye."

"Wait a minute. Let me stop the car. You wanna get killed?"

Mario moved the car into the shade of an oak tree and waited with his foot on the brake. "Take care, man, allí te watcho, and if you ever want to get together, I'm sometimes around the Market Basket over on North Broadway."

Fausto opened the door. With his hand raised and one foot still in the car, he listened. "Can you wait for me?"

Mario removed his dark glasses and glanced across the level grass toward the main road. Behind the barbecue pits a barechested man was throwing a frisbee to his Doberman. "Okay, but hurry up," Mario said. "I don't like this place."

Fausto discovered the shepherd sitting on the edge of a culvert beside the playground swings. The slender young man was popping roasted corn kernels in his mouth while his animals grazed around the water fountain. He looked up quizzically at the stranger in the cape, then held out his red, cloth pouch with the corn. Fausto shook his head and pointed to his teeth. "I can't," he said, first in English, then explained in Spanish about the piñón shell that once slipped between a bridge wire and his molar. The shepherd dug into another pouch and offered up a handful of coca leaves, along with a piece of chalky white stone. Fausto politely refused, adding he preferred cigarettes.

At the sound of the car horn the alpacas propped their heads erect and tested the air. The young man winced.

"Don't be afraid," Fausto said, stepping next to the culvert. He clasped the timid, moist hand and introduced himself. "I know how you feel."

The shepherd waited until the long, woolly necks were again lowered to the ground, then spoke gently, as if the trees should not hear, as if the wind would take his words and change them into nothing. His name was Marcelino Huanca and he had somehow become lost. Fausto recognized several Quechua words and two or three archaic phrases in Spanish, but the gist of Marcelino's story was clear: he had wandered from the usual pastures, drifted over the mountain pass and forgetting how late it was had descended into a valley of blinding lights, strange noises and smooth, flat fields as hard as stone.

Again the car horn, loud, insistent.

Fausto palmed the back of Marcelino's poncho and invited him home. "I'll help you . . . ."

"And them?" Marcelino motioned to the herd; the earflaps of his cap waved like wilted bird wings.

Fausto was about to suggest the alpacas come too when he heard the car door slam and Mario's shrill voice calling him. The shepherd jerked to his feet and rushed at the animals, shooing them up through the brush and trees. In seconds they were gone, leaving Fausto in a sudden, dusty silence.

Mario jogged into the clearing. "Let's go! I can't wait no longer." His face glistened and slick strands of hair drooped over his ears.

"I found him," Fausto said, still gazing at the spot where Marcelino had disappeared. "He'll be back . . . ."

"Vámonos."

"Wait . . . just a few more minutes. Somebody has to help him. You know, he came all the way from Peru."

"I don't care if he came from China. You ain't gonna help nobody if some cop sees us. Them vatos train their dogs around here. Man, them dogs'll rip you up so bad you'll look like chorizo."

Fausto reluctantly slid off the corrugated culvert and followed Mario to the car. As they reached the curb, a pink frisbee sailed across the street and bounced between Mario's feet. The big Doberman leaped off the lawn, followed by Mr. America, barefoot and smiling.

"Shit," Mario said, turning limp.

Fausto quickly retrieved the frisbee and held it for the drooling, opened jaws. Instead of taking it, the dog growled and sniffed at the two men.

"Chorizo," Mario whispered, "chorizo, man."

Fausto threw the frisbee, and the dog bounded away.

"Very good," the barechested man said, swinging the heavy chain leash from his wrist. "He usually bites strangers."

"That's nice," Mario said. "Does he like arms or legs?"

"No kidding," the muscle man said. "You two did alright."

"Is your little test over?"

"Hey, don't get sore. He's really pretty good when you get to know him."

"Yeah? Well, I know some dudes that like to shoot dogs, even good ones."

"Mario, don't be rude," Fausto said, stepping between the two. "The boy didn't mean what he said. A little scared, that's all." Fausto coaxed Mario to the car, and the two got in just as the Doberman dropped the frisbee by the driver's side.

"Listen, kid. I don't need this dog to give you a lesson. I could do it right now. And if it weren't for your old man being so nice, I'd bounce you around like a tennis ball."

Mario stared at the wet, muscular tits in the window. "Is that all?"

"Just that if I ever catch you in this park again, you won't leave in one piece. Now get the hell out!"

At a safe distance Mario hung his arm out the door and banged a goodbye with his middle finger. On the drive down to the valley Fausto was already planning tomorrow's return to the park. "Can you help me?" he asked, quite confident of the answer.

"Are you crazy!"

"I'll protect you."

"You? No way I'm gonna go back."

Fausto pointed to his house. Carmela was sitting on the veranda reading a newspaper. "I'll see you tomorrow morning," Fausto said calmly. Mario started to grin, then frowned as he saw Carmela drop the paper and run toward the gate.

"Who's that?" Mario asked. "Get out! Hurry, get out!"

"Tío, what are you ...." Carmela glared at the strange face behind the wheel.

Fausto pushed himself up from the seat, holding onto the door.

"Tío! That's not Jess!"

"Of course it isn't."

"What's he doing with his car?"

"Mijita, don't get excited. He's my friend." Fausto had barely stood when Mario shot the car forward, tires screaming, the door flapping once before it locked.

"I'm calling the police," Carmela said.

Fausto struggled after her. "Don't, Carmela. Don't do that."

"He's the one that stole the car."

"Don't call, they're after me too."

Carmela stopped.

"Sit down," Fausto said, "I'll tell you what happened." Carmela stood by the screen door, locking her fingers together as her uncle patiently began with his arrival in Lima. Eventually, after much detail, he entered Cuzco.

"Tío, get to the point!"

"You want to hear the whole story?"

"Yes, but hurry up. He could be in Long Beach by now."

Fausto continued, Carmela giving up and sitting by his side on the veranda steps. When he reached the part where the alpacas ran onto the freeway ramp, he waited till the last moment, till they had forced the traffic to stop. Then he ran onto the freeway, single-handedly moved the herd to the side, turned around and waved the cars by. "There, you see? I do something good and they arrest me."

Carmela was silent.

"Mario helped me get away, so you can't call the police."

"Mario? Is that his name? What's his last name?"

"He wouldn't say."

"Tío," Carmela said after a long pause, "how can I put this . . . .
I don't know what they do in Peru or Panama or any of those other
places, but you're back in Los Angeles now, and that kid stole Jess's
car."

"Don't worry, he'll bring it back."

"How do you know?"

"I know, he's my friend."

"I hope you're right . . . because if Jess ever finds out . . . well,
he . . . he'd die if he knew you knew."

"So?"

"Tío, be serious."

"Don't worry, Carmela. Mario will bring the car back. Remember that horse in Mexico? How you got lost, and it returned to the
corral all by itself? The same thing will happen with Mario. You'll
see."

Carmela nodded. She wouldn't admit it to anyone, but that
time on the horse, really a mule, she had sat snugly against the saddle
horn and for the first time had sensed the pleasure of orgasm.
Rocking back and forth, her body weak, legs dangling, she had
dropped the reins and let the mule follow its own course. It
happened under a tree while climbing a hill. Her hair caught lightly
on a low, leafless branch, and she grasped the animal's sweaty neck,
hoping to guide it away from the tree. But the mule stubbornly
plodded through the high grass, taking the shortcut up the slope. For
a long while, hours it seemed, she and the mule roamed about
aimlessly. She had been afraid to return, expecting her uncle to
notice some change in her face.

"Let's eat," Carmela said abruptly. She stood and lifted
Fausto's arm. "And pray you're right about the car."

"You pray, I'm too tired."

He followed her into the kitchen and sat by the front window.
"How about some quesadillas?" she asked. "That's all there is."

"Anything, mijita."

"I'll go shopping tomorrow."

Fausto watched her place a large flour tortilla on the skillet.
Then she removed the square vegetable grater from a nail above the
breadbox. Carefully, without losing a shred, she grated a small block
of jack cheese onto the middle of the tortilla. Afterward she walked
to the refrigerator, removed a bottle of milk and began to pour some

in a saucepan.

"I want it cold," Fausto said.

"Doctor Chávez said warm milk."

"Doctor Chávez says that to anybody who's dying. What else can he say?"

"You'll drink it warm. If you can't stay home and rest, at least you'll drink warm milk."

"What if he told you to give me poison? Would you do it?"

"Sure."

"You would?"

"Why not? Unless you were allergic or something."

"Mijita, poison kills people."

"I know, but isn't that what you're doing walking all over town?"

Fausto shrugged and turned to the window. He lifted the curtain and looked at the gray, smoggy reflection in the night sky. "Carmela, would you mind if someone else lived with us?"

"Who?"

"The man I told you about . . . the one with the alpacas."

"That's a silly question. Of course not." Carmela set the hot quesadilla and a glass of milk on the table. "Now eat your dinner."

FIVE

The next morning the cloud of snow gathered itself beyond Pacoima and slowly blew eastward. By morning it had reached the Glendale Boulevard bridge and for a while hovered over the rush-hour traffic. Cars, trucks and buses stopped. Suddenly a woman wearing a purple jump suit and straw pith-helmet propped her scooter against the curb and began throwing snowballs at anyone within range. Soon everyone was flinging snowballs. Then the cloud moved on, occasionally following the course of the LA River.

Fausto was changing the parakeet's newspaper, carefully folding the edges to fit the tray. The bird clung to the side and pecked at itself in the mirror.

"I think he needs a tranquilizer," Carmela said, drying her hands on the dishtowel. "Don't you think he's jumpy?"

"He's happy." Fausto placed the cage on the portable TV table next to the radio, then raised his arms to embrace the air and shuffled around the kitchen, keeping time with the Mexican polka. His cape, which he had ironed himself with only one brown, burned spot, dangled from his neck like a court jester's bib. Carmela usually joined him, but this morning it seemed as if he had a partner. He also moved with a spryness she hadn't seen in years.

"You and Tico-Tico," she said as he careened toward the sink.

"Dance?"

"No, Tío . . . . Aren't you getting tired?"

"A little."

Watching him carry his frail body gracefully about the room, humming to himself, Carmela remembered the children across the street. The two girls had called him Toto. She and Fausto had seen them run away apparently giggling over the new name. "Toto? What does that mean?" Fausto had asked her. She had said the girls should be taught some respect, but her uncle had insisted it was a good name.

Carmela wiped the crumbs from the table. Now with that cape everyone will call you Toto. What a name, what a silly name.

After the polka Fausto dropped onto a chair to catch his breath. The two were quiet as the radio announcer briefly mentioned the snow cloud. It was simply described as a "curiosidad" wandering over their neighborhood.

"Come on," Fausto said, hurriedly slipping on his garden shoes. "Let's go find it."

"You believe that? It's probably a joke."

"Only one way to find out . . . ."

"Tío, your shoelaces."

Fausto bent down and fidgeted with the laces. "No puedo."

"I'll tie them," she said, sensing an odd excitement in his voice. Fausto wished he had his staff, but that would have to wait. He hurried down the front steps with Carmela at his side. "Look everywhere," he instructed. "Don't miss a thing." At the corner they saw Mrs. Rentería coming toward them, pumping her arms as if she were swimming against the current. "Fausto! Fausto!" she cried.

"¿Qué pasa, señora?"

The woman held onto Carmela for balance. "Fausto!"

"Say it, señora."

Her wide bosom swelled and she looked behind as if she were being chased. The gray sweater sagged over her belly, and the black, matron shoes were wet and puckered.

"I know, señora," Fausto said. "It's the snow, verdad?"

"¿Cómo sabes?"

"The radio." Looking up through the web of telephone wires and tree branches, Fausto scanned the sky.

"But I just saw it," Mrs. Rentería said, nodding to Carmela. "With my own eyes!"

"Where?" Fausto asked.

"In my backyard. I was hanging out clothes, then everything turned white. Así . . . whoosh!"

"Is it still there?"

"It's melting."

"I mean the cloud."

"No sé. I dropped everything and ran."

"Well, I wouldn't worry about it. A little snow won't hurt your clothes."

"And my flowers?"

"They'll grow again."

Mrs. Rentería, glancing around, excused herself and moved on down the sidewalk.

"Where you going?" Fausto called.

"To Cuca, she'll know what to do."

Years ago Cuca impressed everyone when she predicted the river would overflow. She was off by a year and two weeks, but her shaky reputation as a fortune teller was made. Previously she had been respected only for her healing, but now her clients often brought her impossible requests, like raising the dead or making an Iris bloom in winter.

Fausto and Carmela watched Mrs. Rentería bob toward Cuca's house, then they crossed the street and quickly walked the long, sloping block toward the river. When they arrived at Mrs. Rentería's house, the cloud was gone. At the end of the driveway leading to the garage several neighbors watched with worried expressions as their children ran beneath the clotheslines.

"What do you think about this?" Tiburcio asked.

"I don't know," Fausto said. "It's too early to tell."

"It won't hurt the children, will it?"

"A little snow?"

"It's so strange," Carmela said, nudging the edge of the patch with her toe. "Shouldn't it be everywhere? All over?"

"It's choosy," Fausto explained. "You notice it didn't touch the avocado tree. That would kill the fruit."

"That's right," Tiburcio said. "I guess it won't hurt the kids either."

Fausto gazed over the rooftops to the sky, which for the first time in months suggested blue. "Come, Carmela. I have a feeling the cloud went over the fence to the river."

The neighbors followed him out of the yard. In the street more joined the group. At the end of the block they rushed past the dead-end barrier, climbed the levee and halted at the top of the bank. Fausto pointed. "Over there!"

The cloud had settled on the river bed, resting on the rocks. A wide streak of snow covered the concrete bank, stretching along the bottom to the other side.

Mrs. Noriega, her stockings rolled down to her ankles, stepped to the bank's edge. "It doesn't hurt to call the priest."

"What for?" Fausto said. "Leave it alone."

No one moved as they studied the cloud. Once it shouldered itself onto a pile of larger rocks, but nothing more. Carmela bit her nails, the fishman Smaldino wondered how his cod would keep in snow, and Tiburcio's son Robert noisily puffed air into three wads of bubble gum. When Mrs. Rentería reached the levee, everyone turned. "Cuca says it's too early to talk about the snow," the winded spinster announced.

"Why?" Tiburcio asked. "Isn't she supposed to know about these things?"

"She says she hasn't had her coffee."

Fausto had decided. He stepped to the edge, shrieked a sort of charging yell, leaped into the air and skidded down the slope to the

59

bottom. Carmela froze, expecting catastrophe. But after a brief silence, Fausto sat up and signaled to the children. In seconds they plunged down, whooping and hollering. The shouting must have wakened the cloud, for no sooner had the children reached Fausto than the gray shadow skipped off to the far bank. With increasing speed it swerved from side to side, eventually dipping under the Pasadena Freeway and disappearing at the bend. Fausto turned to the children. "What are you waiting for?"

They played most of the day, sledding on flattened cardboard, throwing snowballs, shaping snowmen, building castles. Whole families came and many people left their jobs. Someone started a small fire to dry wet socks and pants. Smaldino's eldest boy bought a pair of splintered Salvation Army skis for two dollars and rented them for five cents a ride. And Mrs. Rentería hauled out an old card table and made snow cones with three flavors of syrup.

All this time Cuca had remained at home. The snow had been a blessing for her business, especially fortunes and astrology readings. By early afternoon she had done four of each, plus a half-dozen cures based on some use of snow.

For his part, Fausto seemed to have forgotten the snowfield of Peru and his shepherd friend in the hills. Most of the morning he was seated in a portable lawnchair, legs outstretched, watching the children and soothing his joints with snowpacks. It wasn't until Jess slapped him on the back that he remembered Mario and the car.

"You'll never believe it," Jess said excitedly. "They found my car. This morning, over in Culver City."

Carmela glanced at Fausto. "In one piece?"

"Perfect. The tank's about empty, but that's all. I was sure the engine'd be torn up."

Carmela put an arm around Jess's waist. "Great, I'm glad nothing happened to it."

"Yeah . . . but what's weird is that it was in Culver City. They ripped it off in El Sereno. That's twenty miles away. I don't know . . . ." Jess looked at the snow for the first time. He was Carmela's height, but his strong jaw and wide, handsome face gave him the appearance of a larger man. "They said everyone was down here. What'd you do, have a truck dump a load?"

"It snowed," Fausto said.

"Sure, how much did it cost?"

"It did, Jess," Carmela said. "This little cloud came by and . . . . Well, ask anybody."

"Yeah . . . . Hey, let's drive around some. I got to test

everything out. Okay?"

"I can't, Jess. It's Saturday, and I told Tío I'd stay with him today."

"A couple hours. What do you say, Mr. Tejada?"

"You can call me Fausto."

"I'll bring her right back."

"Go on, mijita. I'm not going anywhere."

"Jess will take me shopping," Carmela said. "Right?"

By evening the children had climbed out of the slush, and Fausto remained alone on the levee. Someone had loaned him a blanket and he lay on the lawnchair with only his face and two fingers visible, quietly drawing the last life out of a cigarette stub. Tomorrow he would go to the park and find Marcelino. Pobrecito, he was probably out of food by now. Too bad he hadn't been at the river. The snow wouldn't have been new to him, but maybe he would have liked one of Mrs. Noriega's enchiladas. Or a little soup.

"Tío? Are you still here?" Carmela approached the dark figure by the bank's edge, careful not to slip on the water or trip on the snowmen. She touched his shoulder. "Ready to go home? Jess has the car loaded with groceries."

"I'm ready." Fausto sighed and pulled off the blanket. "Maybe it'll snow tomorrow . . . ."

"The kids would freak out."

"Frick . . .?"

"They'd like it, Tío. Nobody'd go to misa, and Father what's-his-name would get all pissed."

Carmela took the folded chair and helped him down the asphalt bank to the street. Jess drove them to the house, helped Carmela unload the groceries from the trunk, then waited for her to finish shelving the cans, vegetables and frozen meats. He sat at the kitchen table with Fausto.

"That smell," Carmela said, "there it is again." She looked in the bottom of the pantry, through the grate to the sand under the house. "No, it's not coming from there."

"I told you, it's chicha. They drink it in Peru . . . something like pulque."

"Tío, be serious. Why would that . . . chichi be here?"

"Chicha."

"Smells like something rotten," Jess said, opening the window.

"Mijita, that's chicha. How could I forget it?"

"Alright," Carmela said, putting on her apron, "both of you go

61

wash. And when you're done . . . Jess, you can peel the potatoes and carrots."

"Hey, I can't do that."

"If you want dinner, you better. Tío, can you look around? Maybe you forgot some food in the living room. It's probably those beans I made you last week."

"I ate them."

"Remember the fish I found under the sofa? Tío, if you don't like something, tell me." Carmela watched them leave, thinking she'd much rather be at her desk in the Hall of Records, no matter how boring the figures were.

When the two men returned, she accused her uncle of smoking pot in the utility porch. "It's that kid you were with, isn't it? Is he a dealer or something? Is that why the police were after you?"

"Mijita, what are you talking about? Pot? What's that?"

"Marijuana! Look in the porch, it's all over the floor."

Jess reached the porch first. He knelt and picked up a leaf, smelled it, licked it and finally chewed the tip. "It's something else," he said.

Fausto crinkled a few of the hard, dry leaves in his hand. "I can tell you without even smelling," he said, smiling. "It's coca."

"Really?" Jess said. "Hey, Carmela, he's all right."

"But it's not mine," Fausto said. "It belongs to my friend."

"Tío, you can be arrested for having this stuff. Isn't it like cocaine?"

"Mijita, help me sweep it up. We'll save it for when he comes back."

"Who's coming back?"

"I told you, my friend. Not Mario . . . ."

"Who's Mario?" Jess asked.

"Never mind," Carmela said.

". . . no, not Mario, but Marcelino . . . Marcelino Huanca."

SIX

Jess was downstairs watching the wrestling matches on television, Fausto was in bed counting his varicose veins, and Carmela had just flushed the toilet.

The shadow behind the shower curtain lowered itself into the bathtub.

"Tío! Jess!" Carmela yanked up her panties and sidestepped to the door. She yelled again at the top of the stairs, then ran into Fausto's room.

"Don't move!" Fausto whispered. He was on the floor fingering the lint under the bed.

"Tío, something's in the bathtub."

"Carmela, can you turn on the light? One of them got away."

She flipped the switch and glanced into the hallway. "Hurry, Tío!"

Fausto crept forward. "There you are, come to daddy . . . that's it, come to daddy."

"What is it?" Carmela asked, peeking under the bed.

With his index finger and thumb, Fausto picked up the lint and carefully placed it on his right leg. "I was afraid you'd step on it. Sometimes they crawl off the bed and get lost."

"Something's in the bathtub . . . ."

"Varicose veins are like that." He patted the flacid, pallid skin and dropped the pajama leg. "A ver . . . help me up. It's probably a cucaracha."

"No, it's big."

"Where's Jesús?"

"Watching tv . . . . Jess! Come up here!"

Jess was determined to go the limit with Monster Mulhoon, the Giant of the Ozarks. "Just a minute," he answered, then saw the flying kick coming, heard the crack, and his spine broke like a saltine cracker. He fell to the carpet and waited helplessly for another Mulhoon trick.

"Jess!"

"Alright, I'm coming." Rolling on his side, he socked the armchair cushion, ducked under the hairy eye-gouge and whopped the Giant on the ear. Mulhoon tumbled onto the coffee table. Jess bent over his victim, tweaked the handlebar moustache and skipped away toward the stairs.

"What's the matter?" he asked at the bathroom door.

"Something's in there," Carmela said. "Can you take a look?"

"Well, what is it? A spider, snake, what?"

"Bigger . . . . Jess, I'm scared."

"Why don't we call the fire department?"

Fausto elbowed past his niece and pulled back the shower curtain. Marcelino smiled, one hand in the soap dish.

Carmela stepped back. "What is it?"

"Marcelino, stand up."

"Smells funny," Jess said. "Why don't you make him take a bath?"

"Breathe through your nose," Carmela said, waving a hand.

"Marcelino, please stand up."

"Tío, is this your friend?"

"Yes, he can sleep in my room."

"Is he the cocaine guy?" Jess asked.

Fausto was busy splashing cologne on the red and black poncho. "There," he said. "Marcelino Huanca, I'd like you to meet my niece Carmela and her friend Jesús. "

"Tío, it's Jess."

Marcelino averted his eyes, nodded and followed Fausto to the bedroom.

Jess poked Carmela. "Ask your old man if he speaks."

"You ask him, I'm tired of sticking my nose in."

"See if he's got more of those leaves."

"No, Jess. My uncle's not feeling well. Leave him alone. Tío, let me bring up the cot. You can't both sleep in the bed."

"We're fine, mijita. Just close the door."

"You sure? I'll get you another blanket."

"No, go on. I'll call you if I need something. And mijita?"

"Yes, Tío."

"Turn off the light."

The fog rippled through the streets like an unbreaking wave, caressing houses and trees, pigeons and drunks, with the same wet chill that began to crawl over Fausto's hands, dipping into the joints, swirling about each knuckle as if pain were a gift.

"I won't stay here, Marcelino. This is the worst place in the world to die. Anyplace but here."

"Señor, we could go back to my home."

"Yes, I'd like that . . . . But I'm afraid it's impossible. My energy's gone. Look at me, all shriveled up like a peanut."

"And my alpacas?"

"Don't worry, I can still go to the park."

"Now?"

"No, it's better if we sleep first. Besides, you can't see anything with all this fog."

Earlier Marcelino said he had lost the herd. The animals had scattered when the helicopter descended into the clearing between the trees. A man had chased him down through the cover of dry grass and nettles until he reached the steep cut of earth above the freeway. Marcelino escaped by sliding to the bottom of the cliff, which banked up against the Los Feliz barber shop and theater. At that point, bruised and punchy, he had nowhere to go but to Fausto's.

"Buenas noches," Fausto said. "A little rest, y quién sabe? Maybe I'll live another day." He finished rubbing the Ben Gay on his hands, turned on his side and fell asleep.

But Marcelino could not sleep. In the darkness of the strange room he listened to the pigeons cooing, to pieces of drunken songs, to the constant, eerie cries of rusty freight car wheels. Squatting by the dresser, he watched the silhouette of the old man's chest rise and fall. Now and then Fausto would cough something into a wad of Kleenex, then drop back onto his pillow. Hours later a rooster broke the air with the first crow of morning.

"It's time," Fausto whispered, clearing his throat. "Marcelino?"

"Señor?"

"Ah, I thought you had left." Fausto pulled the lamp cord. Today's mission would require a certain touch, something commanding respect, something that would mark him as a gentleman. What could he wear? His slippers were nothing extraordinary. His trousers, even when ironed, weren't worth a second look. But a hat? Yes, that would do it. Since he no longer had a staff, a hat would do nicely.

From the closet he brought out a ragged garden hat, dusting the brim and placing it on his head at a smart tilt. In the dresser mirror it looked like a pith helmet, and who would know it was made of straw? Marcelino waited patiently while his host fumbled with his other clothes.

"Can you tie this?" Fausto said, holding out the tassles of his cape. "I can't see too well."

In the kitchen he toasted two slices of rye bread, then prepared a saucepan of double-strength Sanka. Before sitting to eat, he uncovered the birdcage and poured more seed into Tico-Tico's feeder. Marcelino knelt by the cage and very softly amused the bird with his flute. Tico-Tico stretched his legs and opened one eye.

"I'll give him some anís," Fausto said. "That usually helps." He removed the crystal liqueur bottle from the cupboard shelf over the refrigerator, touched the closed beak with a wet finger and dropped a spoonful of anís in the water dish. The parakeet hopped off the top bar and onto the dish rim. For a moment he eyeballed his reflection, then opened the bluish beak and tried to squeak.

"Good boy, Tiquito!" Fausto explained the bird had a growth removed from his throat, and ever since he hadn't spoken a word. "But I think he's using that as an excuse," Fausto said, shuffling to the stove. He lit the oven, leaving the door down. "Please, eat. I have to wake up my legs first." Fausto hiked the kimono above his trousers, and the heat quickly penetrated the material on his thighs and buttocks. Then he turned around to warm his other side. Marcelino meanwhile squatted by the cage, chewing the bread and sipping Sanka.

"I suppose you're right," Fausto said. "What good are chairs if you can't use them? I wonder what we'd do without chairs?" Dropping the kimono hem, he sat down at the table and stared at the gray reflection between the curtains. Beyond his face a woman's stooped figure in black struggled by on the way to six o'clock mass. "Maybe we'd lower the windows . . . ." Fausto watched the woman disappear into the fog. "Marcelino?"

"Señor?"

"Do I look old to you?" Fausto stiffened his back, hoping for a touch of youth at the tip of his chin.

Marcelino studied the pose. "Almost . . . ."

"Almost?"

"Well . . . perhaps not almost. You still have a few years left." Fausto lifted the soggy toast from the cup, slurping loudly. "A few . . . a few days, verdad?"

"If it bothers you so much, why don't you try my uncle Celso's remedy?"

"Does it hurt?"

"Only if it doesn't work. Then you die like everyone else."

"Nothing works."

"They say it puts new life back in the old skeleton."

"What about the rest of me?"

"Oh, that too."

"So what do I do?"

"If I remember . . . Celso started with a bag of stones all about the same size. You take the stones and make a little pile. You make it as high as you can, until you are sure no more stones can be put on top without falling. Then, and this is the hardest part . . . if you truly believe you can, you place one more stone on top. If it stays and does not fall, you will be as strong as that last stone. Nothing can make you fall."

"What if there's an earthquake, a little wind or something?"

"Then everything will fall."

"Everything?"

"Everything."

Fausto was silent while he finished his Sanka. "I don't know," he said, carrying the cup and saucer to the sink, "it sounds risky. Tell me, did this remedy work for your uncle?"

"No, the rain washed the stones away."

"Of course."

"They say he died a happy man. The birds had already taken his eyes, but you could still see the smile."

They were quiet. Fausto tapped the table edge with one finger, then scooped up the bread crumbs and dropped them in the cage. "You know, Marcelino, I like that. But my pile of stones will be under the house . . . in case it rains."

Daylight had pushed through the fog, illuminating Fausto's little tower of life. Marcelino congratulated him and said it had taken more than skill. Courage did it.

"And no cheating," Fausto added. "It was just like you said, I had to believe I could do it."

The two slapped the sand from their hands, brushed the moist grains from their clothes and started the trek to Elysian Park. After what seemed like hours, they left Stadium Way and followed a narrow, potholed street without curbs. At the first bend in the road they were met by two men resting behind a barricade. The men were young, black and wore tan uniforms with ironed creases running from their shirt pockets to their trouser cuffs. The tallest had just finished telling how his wife could pick up the highway patrol on a tooth.

"The dentist put this piece of steel in, and now she wants him to turn it off!"

The short man laughed and turned the radio dial to another station. Out of the corner of his eye he saw the two strangers turn the bend. "Check this."

Fausto approached first, Marcelino remaining a few steps behind. "Gentlemen, good morning," he said, tipping his hat.

"Morning to you," the tall man said with a wink.

"May we pass?"

"Depends. You friend or foe?"

"Foe?"

"Foe, huh?" The tall man glanced at his partner. "Should we arrest him?"

"I mean *friend!*" Fausto blurted.

"In that case . . . . Suppose you follow the road, my good man."

"Yes, thank you. Come, Marcelino, we're safe."

The wooden barricade slid back, and the two guards snapped a salute and waved them on.

"Why are they so black?" Marcelino asked after they had walked a short distance.

"You've never seen black people?"

"No. My cousin Aurora is very dark, but she's never been black."

"Well, don't believe what you see, they don't paint themselves. That's the way they were born, black."

"The burn they have . . . it doesn't hurt?"

"No, it doesn't hurt."

Fausto went on to explain how the first Europeans in the Americas actually thought some of the people they saw on the shore had tails and lived in trees.

"Tails?"

"Long ones too . . . here, between your legs."

"Señor!"

"It's true. You know, they even said some people were green and lived in the ground. That was Ponce, he wasn't very smart."

"In the ground? How could a man breathe?"

"I don't know, Ponce liked to make up stories. But if you think that's strange, in Patagonia they said they saw giants with huge feet. And during the winter when there was no food, the giants ate their children."

"Those are crazy men's stories."

"I know, but this world is full of crazy people."

They entered the city through the main arch. People, mostly black, crowded along the walls and in the passageway. Marcelino stopped to watch a dice game. Behind the players a large mulatto raised a chicken by its neck. Beside him another man unraveled a thick snake. And over there, Fausto explained, that woman is selling her daughter.

"But why?"

"For money."

Marcelino gazed at the other black faces. Some had scars and they spoke words he could not understand. He would have liked to touch their skin and hair.

"Come," Fausto said, "let's see what's inside."

They stepped between the squatting bodies and passed under the arch. Inside the city wall they faced a nearly empty plaza. Fausto hesitated, inspecting the fresh, evenly spread sand. The smell of paint filled his nostrils, and looking to one side above the wall, he noticed a telephone pole disguised as a palm tree.

"Where are we?" Marcelino asked.

"I don't know . . . Colombia . . . Trinidad . . . Santa Marta, I don't know. I thought I could recognize something, but everything's a little different . . . ."

At the other side of the plaza a group of shirtless blacks emerged from a barnlike building followed by a white man on horseback. When the group had gathered itself on the street, the blacks crowded close and listened to the white man. Now and then the mob would shout and wave their machetes in the air, the wild glints of steel driving terror into Marcelino's eyes.

"I think we're expected," Fausto said, calmly adjusting the pleats of his cape. "Could you play something with your flute? It might impress them."

Marcelino lifted the hollow cane to his dry lips but could only manage a timid rasp. They walked toward the group. As they reached the plaza's center, a baldheaded man in a bushjacket hollered from the top of the barn. The horse reared and wheeled into the machetes. The bushjacket shouted again, this time into a megaphone.

"English," Fausto said. Marcelino nodded and continued rasping.

"Get those guys out!" the bushjacket screamed. "What kind of costumes are those anyway?"

The horse charged into the plaza. Fausto waited, then raised a hand before the animal could stop. "Sir, let me introduce myself . . . ."

"Get out of here! Can't you see . . . ."

"And whom do I have the pleasure of addressing?"

The rider dismounted and took Fausto by the hand. "It's late," he said, "and everyone wants to be the big cheese. But not now, okay, old buddy?"

"Sir, I am Don Fausto Tejada, and this is my companion Marcelino Huanca."

"And I'm Marlon Brando. Listen, go wait in that building. When the revolution's over, you can come out."

"Revolution?"

"Yeah, we've got one more take to do, then it's all over. Now be a good fellow and wait in there."

"Certainly .... I believe I was mistaken about our location, Marcelino. No more music."

"Take care of them," the man shouted to a woman in cut-off Levis and sneakers. Fausto and Marcelino were shown into a smoke-filled room and told to sit. Around them were racks of clothes, small tables with mirrors, and in the middle next to the cots a table with beer, ice, gin and Dixie cups. Most of the crowd was by the table.

"Wrong period," the woman said to Fausto. "We're doing seventeenth century." She turned to Marcelino. "And that's out, definitely. Anyway, we're not shooting Indians."

"He's Peruvian," Fausto said.

"You don't say?" Spreading a wet armpit, she drew a circle in the air with her cigarette. "I'm from Oklahoma myself .... Why are you looking at me like that?"

"Would you mind? I haven't smoked all day."

"Sorry. I know, the first day's a bitch."

"No, I'd like one, please."

"Oh, sure. Take this." She lit another for herself. "Where do you guys fit in?"

"Nowhere, they won't let us leave."

"I thought you were the beggars. They've got a few of those, you know."

"Madame, do we look like beggars?"

"Well, I'm a whore."

"Madame, we are visitors."

"I also play a flower girl. I did that yesterday."

"I hoped we would be treated with respect."

"Don't get so touchy. One day a beggar, another day a soldier. And don't call me *madame*. I'm just a whore."

"Miss, under whose orders are we being held?"

"No one's *holding* you. Relax, have a drink."

Fausto had puffed down to the filter. Marcelino, clinging to the edge of the cot, watched the strange figures around him. They were all giants, even the women, except for the bearded midget exercising alone in the corner. Marcelino stared at the squat, stumpy legs and wondered why the man had not grown up.

The woman drew back, tilted her head sideways and squinted. "You know, there's something about you two, something really authentic. But don't let casting catch you in those outfits." She rubbed the greasepaint from her nose and moved away. "Stick around, I'll see you later."

Fausto grew restless; he was concerned about Marcelino. His friend had now retreated into his poncho, dazed from the smoke, noise and a throbbing fear that someone was about to knock him to the floor. His lips quivered and his eyes were closed.

"Let's go," Fausto whispered. While no one was watching, the two authentics rose and slowly walked toward the brass-handled doors. Outside, the revolution had started. "Stay close to me, Marcelino. And whatever you do, don't get yourself killed."

They left the building and pressed through the storm of shouting, flailing bodies. Suddenly the megaphone cried, "Cut!"

But the fight had started, already sweeping men and horses into a blind frenzy which could only end in victory or defeat. The rebels were falling, blood spurted on the clean sand, the plaza was lost, they were surrounded, and the voice above kept yelling, "Cut! Cut! Cut!"

Marcelino tripped on a fallen horse and started to get up.

"Stay down!" gurgled a man with a lance in his stomach; the blood spilled from his mouth. "You're dead," he said, slumping to the ground.

Marcelino leaped up and rushed after Fausto. A line of men in blue coats and shiny, black hats charged out of the arch. "That way," Fausto said. He clutched Marcelino's hand, and the two stumbled off the set, underneath the prop braces, escaping into a portable restroom. For a long while they huddled together, listening to the gunshots and shouts of battle.

"I think we're safe," Fausto said. "Let's go."

The fugitives fled through the parking lot, past the snackbar and into the woods. It wasn't long before they reached the television antenna overlooking the park. The fog had turned to smog, revealing the dim outline of the upper city walls. The two men leaned against the tall Cyclone fence.

"I'm sorry," Fausto said, his chest heaving with harsh, brittle noises. "It was a trap. I should have known when I saw the telephone pole . . . . Cartagena has charm, and they treat visitors with respect."

Marcelino removed his chullo cap and wiped his forehead. "Why were they fighting?"

"They're making a movie."

"What's that?"

"It's a picture of people who move."

"They talk too?"

"Everything, they do everything we do . . . even fight."

The nightmare swirled in Marcelino's head; he saw the midget lifting barbells, the dying man spewing blood, the machetes hacking at the blond, blue giants.

"But there's a difference between them and us," Fausto said. "We can leave the movie, and they can't. They're trapped."

"Were those men dead . . . the ones on the ground?"

"No, they just look dead."

"And the blood?"

"Dye, red dye."

Marcelino sat on the ground and pulled out his flute.

"Not now," Fausto said. "We're too close."

"I'm calling my alpacas."

"Wait, we'll look for them later. Let me rest a while."

Fausto could count the heart beats; they were loud, convulsive beats. It was as if his heart were angry at not being released. "I've still got you, though. You can't leave me yet."

"What?"

"Nothing, I was talking to my heart. Pobrecito, he can't wait to get out."

"Señor, have you forgotten?"

"What?"

"The remedy."

"Marcelino, I was going to ask you . . . shouldn't I be feeling something by now?"

"Everyone is different. Sometimes the remedy takes longer with some than others, and sometimes it helps only a part of you . . . your liver, your back, your eyes. It's hard to say."

"But I thought you said my whole body?"

"Señor, I'm not an expert in these things. I say what they told me, and that's all."

Fausto thumbed his temples and reflected on his chances of survival. What could he do with a young pair of legs? Nothing, not if the rest of him were old. A new heart? Silly . . . when his head and yes, loins, were as dry as those leaves on the ground. And if he were all new, fresh and strong as Marcelino here, or Mario, what would he do then? Sell books? Would he marry the rancher's daughter from Chihuahua, would Evangelina die so soon, would he grow old, tired and lonely again? No, none of that, please . . . . Perhaps it would be best simply to have a new brain, or new eyes. Then he could see the world as it should be, if only for a few months, a few days. Yes, I would like that. How I would like new eyes!

"Marcelino, do I have a choice?"

"A choice of what?"

"What part of me will be new."

"It's a matter of luck."

"Maybe nothing, is that it?"

"Maybe nothing . . . ."

Fausto rose with difficulty and gazed at the smog-shrouded horizon some fifty yards away. The gray veil parted, and the little snow cloud emerged, springing nimbly up the station antenna above them. And there it remained, tickling itself red on the aircraft warning light.

"Then again," Fausto said, "maybe I'll be lucky."

SEVEN

That afternoon after Fausto had left Marcelino with the alpacas, Mrs. Noriega's grandchildren discovered David in the dry riverbed. The young man was absolutely dead, the children could see that. For a long time they had watched him from behind the clump of cat-'o-nine-tails. His body lay so still even a mouse, poking into one dead nostril, suspected nothing. The girl approached first, leaving behind her two brothers. David's brow was smooth; his gray-blue eyes were half closed; his hair was uncombed and mixed with sand; his dark skin glistened, clean and wet; and the rest of him, torn shirt and patched trousers, was also wet.

"He drowned," the girl said.

The boys ran over for their first good look at a dead man. David was more or less what they expected, except for the gold tooth in front and a mole beneath one sideburn. His name wasn't David yet; that would come later when the others found out. David was the name of a boy who drowned years ago when Cuca predicted it wouldn't rain and it did and the river overflowed, taking little David to the bottom or to the sea, no one knew, because all they found was a washtub he used as a boat.

"How could he drown?" one of the boys asked. "There's no water."

"He did," the girl said. "Look at him."

"I'm telling!" the other boy said, backing away.

The boys ran across the dry sand and pebbles, up the concrete bank and disappeared behind the levee. Before the crowd of neighbors arrived, the girl wiped the dead face with her skirt hem, straightened his clothes as best as she could and tried to remove the sand in his hair. She raised David's head, made a claw with her free hand and raked over the black hair. His skull was smooth on top, with a few bumps above the nape. Finally she made a part on the right side, then lay his head on her lap.

Tiburcio and the boys were the first to reach her, followed by the fishman Smaldino and the other men. Most of the women waited on the levee until Tiburcio signaled it was okay, the man was dead. Carmela helped Mrs. Noriega first, since it was her grandchildren who had discovered David. Then she gave a hand to the other older women. Mrs. Rentería, who appeared even more excited than the others, later suggested the name David.

For some time they debated the cause of death. No bruises, no bleeding, only a slight puffiness to the skin, especially the hands. Someone said they should remove the shoes and socks.

"No," Tiburcio said. "Leave him alone, he's been through enough. Next you'll want to take off his clothes."

Tiburcio was overruled: off came the shoes, a little water and sand spilling out. Both socks had holes at the heels and big toes.

"What about the pants?" someone asked.

In this way they discovered the man not only lacked a small toe on one foot but also had a large tick burrowed in his right thigh and a long scar running from one hip almost to the navel.

"Are you satisfied?" Tiburcio said.

Everyone was silent. David was certainly the best looking young man they had ever seen, at least naked as he now lay. No one seemed to have the slightest shame before this perfect shape of a man; it was as if a statue had been placed among them, and they stared freely at whatever they admired most. Some of the men envied the wide chest, the angular jaw, and the hair, thick and wavy; the women for the most part gazed at the full, parted lips, the sunbaked arms, the long, strong legs and of course the dark, soft mound with its finger of life flopped over, head to the sky.

"Too bad about the missing toe," Tiburcio said. "And the tick, what about that?"

Mrs. Rentería struck a match and held it close to the whitish sac until the insect withdrew. There were oos and ahhs, and the girl who had combed the dead man's hair began to cry. Carmela glanced at the levee and wished that her uncle would hurry.

They all agreed it was death by drowning. That the river was dry occurred only to the children, but they remained quiet, listening to their parents continue about what should be done with the dead man.

Smaldino volunteered his ice locker, No, the women said: David would lose his suppleness, the smooth, lifelike skin would turn blue and harden. Then someone suggested they call Cuca, perhaps she knew how to preserve the dead. Cuca had cures for everything, why not for David?

"No!" Mrs. Rentería shouted, unable to control herself any longer. "He'll stay with me!" Although she had never married, had never been loved by a man, everyone called her Mrs. out of respect, at times even knowing that word could hurt this small, squarish woman who surrounded her house with flowers and worked six days a week changing bedpans and sheets at County General. "David is mine!" she shouted for all to hear.

"David?" Tiburcio asked. "Since when is his name David? He looks to me more like a . . . ." Tiburcio looked at the man's face. ". . . a Luis."

"No, señor!" another voice cried, "Roberto."

"Qué Roberto — Robert!"

"Antonio."

"Henry."

"Lupe!"

Alex, Ronnie, Armando, Trini, Miguel . . . . Everyone had someone.

Meanwhile Mrs. Rentería left her neighbors who one by one turned away to debate the issue. For a while she knelt beside David. Then she stood and wrung out the sopping, gray shorts and began slipping his feet through the leg holes, eventually tugging the elastic past the knees to the thighs. Here she asked for help, but the group didn't seem to hear. So with a determination grown strong by years of spinsterhood, she rolled David onto one side, then the other, at last working the shorts up to his waist. The rest was the same, and she finished dressing him by herself.

When the others returned no one noticed the change, for David appeared as breathtaking dressed as he did naked. "You're right," Tiburcio announced, "his name is David . . . but you still can't have him."

About this time Fausto arrived followed by a hip figure in a black, sheeny shirt and starched khakis. Mario had returned the hoe and now helped the old man across the broken glass and rocks. Fausto, winking at his niece, immediately grasped the situation. David was a wetback.

Yes, there was no mistake. Hadn't he, Fausto, brought over at least a dozen young men from Tijuana — one by one, cramped into the trunk of the car? Of course Fausto knew, for even after these men found work, months later they would return to the house dressed in new clothes but always the same type of clothes. Maybe Fausto wasn't too quick to recognize women illegals, but the men, like young David there, were an easy mark.

"How can you tell?" Smaldino asked.

The old man raised his staff and pointed to the gold tooth, the cut of hair, the shirt collar tag, the narrow trouser cuffs, the thick-heeled, pointy shoes. "It's all there. You think I don't know a mojado when I see one?" As a last gesture he closed the dead man's eyes. "Now . . . what will you do with him?"

"Toto," a small voice came from below; the girl pulled at

Fausto's cape. "Toto, can I have him?"

"No, mija, he's too old for you."

Mrs. Rentería repeated her claim, and before the others could object, Fausto asked in a loud voice what woman among them needed a man so much that she would accept a dead man? "Speak up! Which of you can give this man your entire love, the soul of everything you are? Which of you, if not the señora here who has no one?"

The wives looked at their husbands, and the girls and unmarried women waited in awkward silence.

"Then it's settled," Fausto said with unusual authority. "You, Tiburcio . . . Smaldino and you, Mario, take this man to her house."

"Hey, I ain't touchin' no dead man," Mario said.

Carmela stepped forward. "That figures. You'll go around stealing cars, but you won't help your own kind."

"Alright, alright," Mario muttered, "one time and no more."

That evening so many visitors crowded into the small, frame house next to the river that latecomers were forced to wait their turn in the frontyard. Even Cuca, her stockings rolled down to her ankles, had to wait in line.

Mrs. Rentería had bathed and shaved David, clipped his hair and lightly powdered his cheeks. He wore new clothes (Mario's contribution) and sat quietly in a waxed and polished leather recliner. The neighbors filed by, each shaking the manicured hand, each with a word of greeting or a good-natured joke about the first night in bed. And most everyone returned for a second, third and fourth look at this treasure of manhood which might not survive another day of summer heat.

Like all discoveries, it was only a matter of time until David's usefulness would end, till the colognes and sprays would not mask what was real, till the curious would remain outside, preferring to watch through the window with their noses covered, till the women retreated into the yard, till the men stopped driving by for a glance from the street, till at last only Mrs. Rentería was left to witness the end.

Happily this was a solitary business. For several days she had not gone to the hospital, her work was forgotten, and she passed the daylight hours at David's feet, listening, speaking, giving her secrets. And not once did he notice her splotchy hands, the graying hair nor the plain, uninspired face. During the warm afternoons David would take her out, arm in arm, to stroll through the lush gardens of his home, somewhere far away to the south. He fed her candies, gave her flowers and eventually spoke of eternity and a breeze that never dies. At night she would come to him dressed as a dream, a sprig of jasmine in her hair, then lay by his side until dawn, awake to his every whisper and touch.

On the third day Fausto knew the honeymoon was over. The shepherd Marcelino, safe in the park beneath the station antenna, had already raised his flute to sound the first note of mourning.

"Señora," Fausto called at the door, "it's time David left."

Mrs. Rentería bustled out from the kitchen. Her hair was down in a carefree tangle and she wore only a bathrobe. "You're too late," she said with a smile. "He died this morning . . . about an hour ago."

Fausto examined her eyes, quite dry and obviously sparkling with something more than grief.

"He died?"

"Yes," she stated proudly. "I think it was too much love."

The odor of death was so strong Fausto had to back down the steps. "Señora, I'd be happy to take him away for you. Leave it to me, I'll be right back." He turned quickly and shuffled toward the sidewalk.

"Wait," she shouted. "He's already gone."

"I know, but I'll take him away."

"That's what I mean. This little man — chaparrito y con una gorrita — took him just before you came."

"A little man . . .? Wearing a poncho?"

"That's him."

"Está bien, señora, your David will get the best burial possible."

Mrs. Rentería said she insisted on going with him, but Marcelino refused.

"No te apures, we'll take care of him. The body goes, but the soul . . . ."

"I know, his soul is right here . . . in my heart."

"Good, keep him there. Because if you ever lose him, watch out for the other women."

"He'll never leave. You see, I have his word." She pulled a folded scrap of paper from between her breasts and studied the scribbled words.

Fausto nodded, then asked if he should say something special at the burial. "Some prayer . . . a poem?"

Mrs. Rentería answered with a toss of her head, and for a moment her glassy eyes were lost in the distance, somewhere over Glendale. Then she closed the heavy, wooden door, clicked both locks and dropped the blinds behind the big bay window.

But David was not buried. He left Elysian Valley better than when he had arrived. A man so perfect should not be buried, Fausto told Marcelino. And with the shepherd's guidance and using a knowledge more ancient than the first Inca, than the first Tarahumara, the old man painstakingly restored David to his former self. Even the missing toe was replaced.

By late evening the restoration was almost complete. Only one chore remained. Carmela brought the pitcher of water into the yard and wet the dead man's clothes, the same shabby clothes he wore when they found him.

"More water," Fausto said. This time Mario took the pitcher and skipped into the house. He had watched the transformation completely fascinated. David was about his own age, heavier, but he could have been a brother. And ever since Mrs. Rentería had taken him for her own, Mario's admiration for the young mojado's quiet sense of confidence had grown. The vato is cool, Mario thought as he emptied the pitcher over the dead man's body.

Fausto then asked for the egg, a dried quetzal egg Mario had plucked from the Exposition Park ornithology hall.

"What's that for?" Carmela asked.

"Oh, Cuca once told me that you do this"—and here Fausto lightly brushed the egg on the dead man's lips—"and it brings him good luck. I don't believe it, but just in case . . . ."

Fausto stood back and examined his work under the porch light. "Mario, pick him up."

"Hey, man, I thought it was over."

"Almost. Just do as I say."

Mario struggled with the body, finally lifting it over one shoulder. Carmela opened the gate. "Stay here," Fausto told her.

"Tío!" she called after the men had moved into the darkness. "Where you taking him?"

"Further down the river," came the faint reply, "where others can find him."

EIGHT

Later, after Mario and Marcelino had gone, after Jess had taken Carmela to the movies, Fausto quietly engaged his own image of David's coming and going. Did he die of a weak heart, as Mrs. Rentería said? Was the young mojado good because he was dead, or was he dead because he was good? Something must have killed him.

Fausto listened to the sound of his own feeble heart. Reassured, he lit another cigarette and decided the question hardly mattered, since mojados like David would continue coming and going — dead, half-dead or alive — despite what anyone thought they should do. Thousands, hundreds of thousands, were waiting for a taste, a glimpse, of paradise. Or just a job.

Of course, that's it, Fausto thought. If his wife didn't interfere, what better guide could they have than someone, someone like himself, who could tell them about life and death in the United States, who could also bring them across in style. No more hiding, no more climbing the hills like wild dogs.

The operation would be decent, respectable, the plan quite simple. Fausto had been staring at the cracks in the ceiling. The top layer of paint had chipped, leaving half-formed bubbles and jagged hollow spaces that caught the light from the hallway. The slaky surface was covered with vague designs, tiny ridges, plains, valleys, mountains, coastlines.

He studied the map and hoped his ships had found safe harbor. Sturdy ships they were, built of the finest Durango timber. At this moment they were awaiting their commander's arrival in Venice or Malibu, whichever was better. Fausto would order his captains to weigh anchor before the morning tide. Then they would sail to Mexico's western ports and fill the holds with all the hungry, desperate men willing to ship out with only a promise in return.

"Fausto, what are you doing?"

Fausto peeked over the sheet and saw his wife standing in the doorway. "Thinking," he said.

"If you're thinking what I think you're thinking ... stop thinking. You'll never last a day."

"I will too." He watched her approach. "Eva, I've got it all planned."

"Not a day. Remember the time we went to Catalina? You got seasick before the boat left the harbor. I'm telling you, you won't last an hour."

Fausto dropped his head on the pillow. She was right, but it annoyed him that she came after all the preparations had been completed: the provisions, the crews, tourist cards, everything — even a to-whom-it-may-concern scroll which he had signed with great flourish, concluding the message with a coat of arms all his own. Now she has to come. A few more minutes and I would have been driving south-southwest under a full sail, a strong wind at our stern.

Evangelina sat on the bed and reached under the sheet for the cold, knobby hands. "Why don't you stay home and rest like Carmela says?"

"Eva, there's too much to do. And why should I rest? That's all I've done for the last six years."

She touched his brow, then tickled the large, winglike ear. "Don't think about it."

"That's easy for you to say. You're not the one who's dying. But me? How do I know that stone under the house won't fall? It could happen any minute."

"Alright, but stay away from water, entiendes?"

Fausto nodded.

"And whatever you do, take your pills."

"Pills, pills, pills, they're all sugar .... You know, I liked Doctor Ramírez. He gave me cigars."

"Fausto, he's dead."

"I know, but I was thinking it would have been nice if Chávez had died instead of Ramírez."

". . . and don't smoke so much . . . . ."

Fausto turned on his good side and began counting his ribs, fingering each bone as he listened to his wife go on about his slippers, the cold floor, the sudden drafts, his eating and a visit to Doctor Scholl's to have his corns removed.

"By the way," she asked, "where are you going?"

"A little trip . . . not far."

"Where?"

"Méjico?" Fausto whispered.

"Mexico! What about Peru, and I thought you wanted to see Argentina? Those are such nice places."

"I changed my mind. I want to go back to Méjico."

"What for?"

Fausto was silent. He hung a finger around his collar bone and glanced at the map.

"You're hiding something," she said. "What is it?"

He forced a cough and mumbled something about pyramids,

music and Aztec legends, finally asking her if she would like to come.

"Me? No, gracias, I remember the last time. And you think it's changed?"

"I didn't say that."

"No ... you go. See if you don't get diarrhea. I wouldn't be surprised if you came back dead .... But it's your life. Just remember I warned you."

Evangelina leaned over, kissed him on the nose and gave her blessing. Fausto opened his eyes; she was gone. He was glad she hadn't pried it out of him, yet he really couldn't blame her for disappearing at the idea of visiting Mexico. The last time they went she had lost her voice and thirteen pounds. The other trip, taken years ago, had convinced her Mexico was for Mexicans.

They had been there two weeks, driving south from Juárez to Mexico City. At the time the newspapers and the highway were crowded with the cars of the Pan American Road Race, and Fausto's new, '53 Buick had taken an early lead. Along the route thousands of dusty faces craned for a glimpse of the famous drivers, the big circled numbers, the signs, the slogans, the camera crews, a senator, a movie star. There were foreign names and words like Penzoil, Mobil, Firelli and Goodyear; tall men with blonde women; bands in every plaza, and parades of uniformed children waving red, white and green streamers.

Fausto drove while Evangelina contained herself and little Carmela played string games or read comic books in the backseat. Although his Buick was an unofficial entry — only because he wouldn't pay the fee — everyone recognized him. Entering a city, he would sit back proudly and wave to the crowds lining the narrow sidewalks. He had already announced he would give up the prize money; it would go to an orphanage or to a school for the blind. Yes! the papers would scream, it was the driver without the helmet.

The race wasn't the Gran Prix, but it demanded all the skill and courage of a professional, a true champion. This was in his mind as he eased into the Pemex pitstop in downtown Querétaro. He nodded to the mechanics and casually clicked off the ignition. It was almost over, one more leg, victory was practically in his lap.

"Fausto! I told you to stop where it's clean."

"Sorry ... I forgot."

Evangelina had suffered the worst of it. Throughout the race she cursed the brimming bowls, the caked, hole-in-the-floor toilets, the slimy footpads on each side, praying not to slip, trying to ignore the cockroaches in the corners and under mounds of crumpled, dirtied newspaper. And each time there was no way of telling what was behind those doors. Even in the best hotels and restaurants, Evangelina — expecting American whiteness, spotless tile, crisp paper towels, at least soap — would enter and have to balance herself over another wet toilet seat.

"Gente atascada! That's why they are the way they are . . . . Some vacation! You and your ideas . . . . And look at Carmela. If she doesn't get sick from all this filth, it'll be a miracle . . . . See those men against the wall? Orinando, as if they didn't know how to use a bathroom. Now I know why my father wanted to leave this place."

"Cálmate," Fausto said. "We'll go somewhere else." He signaled "no" to the attendant and slowly nosed the lead car into the street.

"Stop there," his wife said as they neared a newer Pemex station. "That looks clean."

By the time the car was alongside the pumps, Fausto had decided to drop out of the race. What's one race? The only losers will be the blind children and the orphans. And what they don't get now, they'll get the next time I win.

He endured the rest of the trip by singing. Alone to himself, or with the mariachis on the radio. Occasionally he joined them in a huasteca, using his falsete until his voice cracked. Carmela said he sounded like a rooster with a cold, while Evangelina, ignoring the coo-coo-roos, clutched her travel brochures and counted the kilometers to the capital.

No, he couldn't blame her. But like his friend said, Mexico has changed. Last year Tiburcio came back from Guadalajara and described the new buildings, the lights, all the cars and the new trailer camps. "I'll tell you, Fausto, it's not like before . . . ."

"What about the restrooms?"

"No problem, our camper has a toilet."

But it was only for his wife that he asked. Fausto himself hardly worried about dirty toilets. What troubled him now were the mojados. He studied the map again. Too bad, the ships would have to return — all that effort for nothing.

The other plan was more risky. Ni modo, he had no choice. Fortunately Tijuana had not changed. The same. Marines and sailors still swarm over and back on weekends, unquestioned, free to come and go as they please.

Fausto climbed onto the empty oil drum and scanned the hundreds of drawn, bony faces. Then he motioned for the tequila. "All of you, listen to me!" he shouted. "Do as I say and I'll take you across."

No one moved.

"Drink!" Fausto shouted. "Drink until you can't walk straight."

A few men tugged at the stiff, new uniforms, some fidgeted with the strange caps. Should they trust the old man? Why was he doing this . . . and for free? Was it poison?

"What are you waiting for?" Fausto asked. "Do you want to see the United States or not?"

The men gazed at the patient, gray sky, or at the neat rows of houses and the green freeway signs beyond the border. Was it for the gold and silver in their teeth?

"Alright," Fausto said, "I'll count to a hundred, and if all these bottles aren't empty by the time I finish, I'm going without you. Find someone else to take you across."

Fausto began counting. At seventy-three the bottles were empty.

"Good. Now follow me."

"Wait a minute," someone said, touching his shoulder. Fausto didn't have to guess who it was. Evangelina loved to have the last say. It was like the time she caught him in bed with another woman. He wanted to say it was only a thought, a dream, harmless, nothing to get excited about. But she knew better. As he was about to give himself up in a sweet, effortless motion, his wife suddenly wedged her leg between him and the young intruder. Fausto squirmed and the woman vanished. "She's really you," he explained. "I just changed your nose a little and gave you bigger hips." Evangelina had smiled, then she placed herself on the old man's fire.

But what was his excuse now? She had seen his army of nobodys — desgraciados, she would say — and how could he convince her they were simply men?

"Is this right?" she asked.

Fausto shrugged. "Who else can help them?" He knew what she was thinking. Whenever she put her lips together like that, tightly, as if she were trapping the words, afraid they might hurt him, whenever she arched her penciled eyebrow, she was thinking he had jumbled his brains.

"Okay," she said, sniffing the alcoholic breeze, "but I hope you know we have too many mojados already."

"Eva, I know what I'm doing. Besides, they can always go back."

At that moment Marcelino danced into the circle of curious

faces. He raised his flute and pointed toward the row of border patrol booths.

"Ay, Faustito," Evangelina said. "You're the one-eyed man leading the blind — el rey Tuerto."

The men, following the lively sound of Marcelino's flute, staggered past the guards, slowly, in two's and three's, sometimes singly, until everyone was across. Everyone except Fausto, who apparently aroused suspicion because of his cape, staff, possibly his dark looks. He was ordered to wait in a small, barren room where his clothes were searched and his body thoroughly examined. "Those are corns," he told the guard, wincing as the metal probe played between his toes. Then in his most exaggerated Oxford English, Fausto recited without a pause the Gettysburg Address, the Pledge of Allegiance and Franklin Roosevelt's death announcement. It was an old trick, but when the guard heard Roosevelt's name, he was convinced. Fausto was given his clothes and told to leave.

"By the way, where d'you learn that?"

Fausto stepped into his wrinkled trousers. "I used to sell books of knowledge . . . and that's one of the things you can learn. I sold a lot of sets that way."

"Well, we're not stupid, you know. You better come up with another number next time."

The march continued north. The only other problem occurred in La Jolla. Marcelino had turned the column of men from the beach and led them through a golf course. The sight of uniformed men, trudging across the greens and down the middle of the fairways soon disrupted play. The male players cursed the extra hazard and stormed off in search of the club manager. However, the women foursomes sat in the shade of their electric carts and eagerly commented on the good looks of this sailor or that Marine. Finally the manager burst through the rough on the seventeenth hole and demanded an explanation. Fausto hurried over. "They don't speak English."

"English hell! I'm calling the police."

"What did I tell you," Evangelina called, setting herself down in a warm sandtrap.

As the manager was about to leave, Mario zipped across the fairway in a flame-red cart. As usual he was dressed in black, this time wearing a purple tie. "Hey, man, you know there's a twelve-time rapist runnin' around your course? Yeah, he could be anywhere. We're just tryin' to catch him." Mario stretched his legs over the front of the cart, leaned back and clasped his hands behind his head. "Go on, tell that to the ladies."

"Who are you?" the manager asked, the pink flush leaving his face.

"He's a friend," Fausto said.

"Are you in charge?"

"Yes."

"Well, do what you have to do, but stay off the playing area . . . at least the greens. Uh . . . what's this rapist look like?"

Fausto hesitated, then looked to Mario for an answer.

"You can't miss him," Mario said. "He's just a little guy . . . 'bout four feet tall."

"Four feet tall?"

"Hey, ese, we ain't got time to waste. The vato's really fast."

"Okay, just hurry up and find him," the manager said, retreating into the rough.

"Thank you," Fausto said to Mario as they left the course.

"Thank Carmela, she's the one that told me where you were."

"How did she know?"

"Says you were talkin' in your sleep . . . something about the beach and La Jolla."

The march continued up the coast. Mario had kept the cart, but Fausto insisted on walking.

"What you gonna do with them vatos?" Mario asked.

"Find them a place to live."

"How you gonna do that?"

"You'll see. I can't tell you now because I'm still thinking about it."

Fausto halted the march somewhere between Leucadia and Oceanside. "Look over there," he shouted to the men.

Beyond Interstate 5, between endless rows of staked tomatoes, hundreds of other illegals waved their short-handled hoes, beckoning to the long line of men. In seconds the newcomers had torn off their uniforms and were rushing across the highway. Fausto watched them embrace, then waited while they talked. Finally one of the men left the field and returned to the highway. He was a young man with an easy, muscular walk.

"Señor?" he said, holding his oversized, Navy-issue shorts at the waist.

"Yes," Fausto said.

"Señor, it's not that I want to complain . . . but we've been talking this over . . . ."

"Go on."

86

"The simple truth is that there aren't enough jobs to go around."

Fausto patted the man's arm. "It's better you discovered this from someone else. Maybe you'll trust me more."

"We all thank you for what you've done."

"Don't thank me yet. You haven't heard what I'm thinking. Go tell the others that if they do what I say, they'll never have to work again." Fausto paused. "No, maybe that's an exaggeration, but at least you won't have to do this kind of work."

The young man was silent for a moment. Then he picked up a dry dirtclod, threw it against the asphalt curb and began to laugh through his teeth.

"How 'bout me?" Mario asked.

Fausto continued. "Tell them to wash themselves, comb their hair, and when that's done . . . ."

"Señor?"

"Tell them to drop dead," Mario interrupted. "How you expect them to live without workin'?"

"You do it," Fausto said.

"I'm different. I was born here."

"Mario, where you were born has nothing to do with it. Now . . . where was I?"

"You were tellin' him to drop dead."

"Hmm . . . . that's not such a bad idea."

"You serious?"

"Look at David. He never complained." Fausto turned to the young wetback. "When we get to where we're going, all of you must pretend you're dead."

"Dead?"

"Don't move your eyes, don't smile, and if you want to use the bathroom, do it when nobody's looking."

"Is that all?" the young man asked.

"No. Whatever people want you to do, you must do it. Some of them will put you in their beds, maybe you'll hang on a wall, or maybe they'll put you in a museum. ¿Quién sabe? But I don't think you'll have to work. You'll be too valuable. And don't worry about food. No one will let you get skinny."

"What about our families?"

"Yeah," Mario said, "what about their viejas?"

"One thing at a time," Fausto said. "First go talk to the others, see what they think."

Fausto's plan quickly spread throughout the fields. Everyone

87

had questions, but no one spoke. They were too excited, and what they said might sound silly. Would they be given days off? Would they be in California or some other place? What if they got tired of playing dead?

"They say yes," the young man announced, still holding onto his boxer shorts. "But they want to know where to wash."

Fausto pointed to Marcelino, who had been waiting in the shade of the overpass, experimenting with a new tune. "Follow him, the man with the flute."

The signal was given, and the army of wetbacks rose and started off toward Los Angeles.

"Mario," Fausto called, gesturing his friend closer, "I think I'll ride with you. I'm tired."

Mario pumped his foot on the cart's accelerator, then hopped off and kicked one of the small, fat tires. "You can't, battery's dead."

Fausto leaned on his staff and sighed, half-expecting his wife to whisper, "I told you so."

"Come on," Mario said. "We can hitchhike."

NINE

"Did you take your pills?" Evangelina asked. The three of them
— Evangelina, Fausto and Mario — had been picked up by two surfers
in a beige and vermillion van. On both sides, under a seascape with a
pink sun dropped on the horizon, were the fine-lettered words
UNITED VANS BERDOO. Fausto moved the beer cans and wet suits
aside and stretched his legs on the shag-upholstered floor. The van
was pitched in the rear so that they looked down on the two heads in
front.

"Well, did you?"

"Leave him alone," Mario said, shaking one of the empty,
twelve-ounce cans, then peering in the hole.

"You stay out of this," she ordered.

Fausto moved his lips.

Evangelina scooted forward and asked the driver to lower the
stereo.

"He can't hear you!" Fausto shouted, "you're dead."

"Then you tell him. I can't hear with all that noise."

"Mario, tell them to lower it."

"That ain't a good idea, ese. They give us a ride, now we're
tellin' them to keep it down. Naw, that ain't cool. They could drop
us off, then where'd we be? Took us two hours to get this ride."

"He's right, Eva."

"What?"

"I took my pills!"

Evangelina appeared satisfied, but the real question, the one she
had never received an answer to, was why was he trying to save the
world?

"Eva, a few mojados isn't the world."

"But why won't you stay in bed and die like everyone else? No,
you have to go off to Peru and God knows where else. And now
you're trying to bring over all these mejicanos."

"What are we? Chinese?"

"But why them? Low-class nothings ... pura gentuza! ...
maleducados ... campesinos ...."

Fausto almost reminded her that he himself had been a street
sweeper when they first saw each other. She and her father had
driven by while he was scraping horse manure from the road. A
young girl, seated stiffly in the back seat, she had waved to him then,
and years later, after the revolution had taken her father, after she

had walked to El Paso with only a suitcase and her good name, they had met again and were married. Fausto often said, and believed, that because of her, he was something more than a nothing. She had taught him everything. She would even have taught him to read, but he already knew. And the most important lessons were his bearing, his speech and his manners. "That's what impresses," she used to say. "It doesn't matter that you're a small man. Speak like a big man."

What could he say? Should he try to explain?

"Campesinos," she said, glancing out the tinted porthole of the van. "Why them?"

"Because . . . I feel sorry for them."

Evangelina was silent. Perhaps she saw him still in the street, looking up and waving to the princess in the back seat of her father's car.

Fausto remembered the last time he had used those words. They had just arrived in Amecameca, a village near the volcano Popocatépetl. Evangelina said she wanted to sit in the sun on the plaza bench.

"Don't get lost," she said.

"We'll walk around. I like these little towns."

"Fausto?"

"What?"

"Take care of Carmela. The last time you two went off she got sick from riding on that mule."

They walked away, entering a cobblestone street tilted toward the middle to form a gutter. "Tío, where we going?" Carmela chewed one end of a purple, corn tortilla, warm and tightly rolled.

"To see if we can rent some horses, like we did in Teocaltiche. Would you like that?"

Carmela nodded and finished her tortilla.

At the edge of the village they asked about horses, but no one seemed to know who might have the animals. Further into the campo they met an old man seated on the rump of a burro following another burro loaded with dry cornstalks. Fausto spoke, and the man pointed with his thumb.

"He has one horse, lives over there, a little ways beyond the arroyo, see over there, you can make out an orchard wall and part of a roof, well, that man has a horse but I don't think he'll lend it to you, he's a very jealous man, he won't even say hello to his neighbors he's so jealous, pobrecito, it's probably because he lost his first wife and two children. We think they died from eating rotten food, but I doubt if you'll get the horse, because ever since she died he won't lend us anything. So you can try, but like I say he won't even say hello to us . . . ."

Fausto thanked the farmer and continued alongside the arroyo. It was powder dry and deeply cut in the sides. At a place where it narrowed, he helped Carmela across and the two climbed the bank to the other side.

The dogs kept barking, even when the woman came out the front doorway and began throwing rocks to scare them away. She was barefoot and kept wiping her hands on her skirt, waiting for Fausto to speak. Several children watched from inside the darkened room. He asked her about the land, the broken, uncultivated land beyond the farm. The mountain seemed to begin its rise just beyond the farm. Before he could say more, she turned and rushed into the house.

A wiry, hollow-cheeked man came out and respectfully asked if he could help them. From their clothes it was obvious the strangers were from the city. Fausto explained they were walking from the village and would like to cross his land.

"Why?" the man asked.

"To see the mountain."

"And you can't see well enough from here?"

"We'd like to get closer . . . . Now, if it doesn't bother you . . . ."

"Please, why not over there? There's plenty of land over there. And if you go that way, it's a much better view. You can't see anything from here."

"But . . . ."

"I'm sorry, you can't cross my land."

"Then we'll go around. Come on, Carmela."

"No! You can't go that way either."

"Listen, no one is going to touch your land."

"Please, it's dangerous. All those rocks you see over there are infested with poisonous spiders. The rocks are covered with holes, and that's where the spiders make their nests."

Carmela watched the man become more and more excited, and although the Spanish words were spoken rapidly, even she could tell the spiders were probably an excuse.

The dogs followed the strangers at a distance to the edge of the cultivated field. The man yelled to them and waved his hat, but his words were lost in the dogs' barking. Fausto found a well-worn path which seemed to lead to the volcanic mounds on the other side of the crude rock-and-cactus wall.

"Don't believe what he said about the spiders, mijita."

"What about the horse?" Carmela had worn her jeans and cowboy shirt.

"Hurry, here he comes again . . . ."

The man ran diagonally across the dry furrows, then stumbled crazily, picked himself up in one motion and leaped over the wall.

"Señor," he said to Fausto, "dos pesitos." He lowered his eyes and extended his hand.

"No, I can't give you money."

The man insisted, pleading as the three walked quickly along the path. Finally Fausto told him to leave.

"Everyone pays me two pesos . . . ."

"I said no."

"Please, understand me. The government says I should watch this land. I have collected at least two pesos from anyone who comes this way. Please . . . I have a wife and children. Did you see them?"

"I don't believe the government asked you to do this."

"Señor, it's obvious you don't live here. If you did, you would know. Look at the sky. It's been this way for months. Not even the beginnings of a cloud. How do you think we live? What do my family and I eat? Please, a little tip, two little pesos . . . ."

Fausto left him squeezing his straw-colored hat. "Who does that baboso think he is? If he wants to beg, let him beg. But why does he lie?"

The two climbed onto the rocks. Fausto looked carefully into the holes and cracks but saw only gravel and clumps of dry grass. They sat down to rest, facing the mountain. For a long while he stared at the wisps of wind-blown snow drawn lightly around the peak, while Carmela threw stones across the field of hardened lava.

"Sit down," Fausto said, "I'll tell you a story." He popped his knuckles and Carmela hunched down to listen.

"It's about a poor man who dreamed he would marry the beautiful daughter of a king. Everyone thought he was crazy for having such a dream, and they laughed. Even the king laughed."

"Why'd he laugh?"

"Well, in those days only a prince could marry the king's daughter. But there was one person who didn't think he was crazy. It was the king's daughter. She had seen the man and didn't laugh. At least not at first. She liked him because he told funny stories and because he made her feel more beautiful than she really was."

"Was she really pretty?"

"Yes, mijita . . . very pretty."

"I bet she wasn't as pretty as Tía Eva."

"Almost . . . . Anyway, one day the king found them together and said he would have the man killed if they were ever caught together again. So the princess and the poor man ran away. But they didn't hide, they weren't ashamed of what they had done. They went to a place where everyone could see them, up to the top of those two volcanoes."

"I only see one."

"It's there, on the other side."

"Did they come back?"

"No, the princess died from the cold."

"What happened to him?"

"Oh, he's still there, waiting for her to wake up."

"Won't he die too?"

"Maybe . . . ."

When they started back to the village, going the long way around the farmer's land, Carmela's sneakers lost their grip on the rock and she slipped into a large pit which was level at the bottom.

"Tío, look what I found!" Three splintered crosses stuck out of the ground at different angles.

"Don't touch them, Carmela. Let me have your hand." Fausto spread himself on the smooth rock, reached for the hand and pulled her up.

"Tío, is someone buried there?"

"Let's go, mijita. Eva will be waiting for us. We've explored enough for one day."

"They always put crosses on dead people?"

"Carmela, don't ask so many questions."

She followed him in silence; they were walking the way they had come. At the house Fausto stopped and called in the open doorway. "Is your husband here?" he asked the woman. "Give him this."

The woman retreated into the room, waving her hand.

"Take the money, it's ten pesos . . . ."

She spat on the hardened dirt floor and turned away. Fausto placed the coin on the ground where she could see it and slowly walked backwards toward his niece.

"Why did you pay him?" Carmela asked when they had left the house.

"I felt sorry for him," her uncle said, almost in a whisper, but what he didn't say was that he was ashamed of himself.

"Is this okay?" the driver of the van said, pulling onto the shoulder.

Mario hung his head between the two bucket seats. "Hey, can't you take us a little more?"

"How far?"

"Just a little ways."

"How far?"

"Oh . . . 'bout ten miles."

"Ten miles! This ain't a taxi. Who's gonna pay my gas?"

"Hey, my old man's had two strokes in the last week. He can't take no more."

"Then how come he's walking around?"

"I'm takin' him to the hospital."

"From Oceanside?"

"Yeah, man . . . he's goin' for some kinda brain transplant."

"Aw, come on! What kind of shit's that?"

"Okay, don't believe me. You wanna kill my old man, you just did it."

"Alright, take it easy. What's the turnoff?"

"Elysian Park. Know where that is?"

"No, but just tell me when to stop."

TEN

When Carmela returned from the drive-in theater, she found her uncle burning with fever. He was in bed, fully dressed, with one moist hand on his staff. As she untied the shoelaces, she noticed his socks were mismatched and his shoes were on the wrong feet. She covered him with the bedspread and rushed out of the house. At Cuca's she banged on the door, then on the bedroom window, until the snoring stopped and the old woman peeked through the blinds.

"Cuca, it's my Tío! He's burning up."

"Okay, okay, let me put something on."

Carmela waited outside, twisting and bobbing as if she had to urinate.

"Fever?" Cuca said, coming out with her sewing bag of medicines. "Well, we'll see." A fragile, white-haired woman with wrinkles running everywhere across her face, Cuca was used to being called in the middle of the night. Sometimes even her worst cures succeeded at night, whereas most of her failures occurred during the day after she had her coffee. She paused at the corner, looked up and tested the overcast sky with her forehead. "Carmela, I know what you're thinking. But he won't die . . . at least not now."

At the house Cuca squeezed a cut lemon into half a glass of water and stirred in two tablespoons of Karo corn syrup. Fausto drank the mixture and asked for more. Cuca refused, saying the remedy called for only half a glass.

"Now," she told Carmela, "go ask Smaldino to bring two buckets of ice."

Carmela left and returned with the fat fishseller; his colorless flannel pajamas had coffee stains at the top and were torn at the crotch. Cuca thanked him for the favor, and Smaldino set the buckets down without a word, turned and stumbled into the wall.

"Carmela, take him home. I don't think he's awake."

When the two had gone, Cuca opened her kit and removed several plastic garbage-disposal bags. She filled them with ice and twisted paper-covered wires around the tops. Then she tucked one bag in each of the sick man's armpits; the third ice-bag she placed on his head.

Fausto opened one eye and winked. "Cuca."

"Yes?"

"It won't work."

"I know, but it makes Carmela feel better."

"If you see my wife, tell her I'm on my way."

"Not so quick, compadre. Take your time . . . al cabo, what's your hurry?"

"You think this is really it?"

"Who knows? It all depends on what you're thinking. The mind usually controls these things. It may last a few days or a few hours. But it's no use worrying about it."

"I suppose you're right."

"If it makes you feel better, I'll tell everyone to come by in the morning. I'm sure they'd like to say goodbye."

"Cuca?"

"Yes."

"Can you put some ice between my legs . . .?"

"Like this?"

"Higher . . . yes, that's it."

Cuca had witnessed many deaths, and it was always a pleasure to see a bit of fire still wriggling around beneath the burned-up coals. She reached for her bag and rose to leave. "Fausto, I'll see you in the morning. Can you wait till I come back?"

"I think so."

"Good. Now rest, and try not to get too excited. The ice should bring the temperature down, but you have to cooperate."

After she left, Marcelino entered. He had been waiting in the bathroom and appeared distressed. "Have you forgotten?" he said. "Nothing can make you fall."

Fausto shifted the ice-bag. "Go away, I'm tired."

"The Mexicans are waiting."

"Tell them to go back. It's no use. I can't help anyone . . . not like this."

"Think of what you could show them . . . a man with all your knowledge."

"Don't flatter me."

"You could show them how movies are made, remember?"

"Marcelino, go watch your alpacas."

"No, I'm staying until you get up."

"How can I get up?"

"Help them."

"Go away, I can't even help myself."

"They're waiting for you in the river."

"Do they look dead?"

"They're trying, they're dying of hunger and cold. Some of them don't even have clothes. There's one man who started shaking so much he said he'd rather be alive than dead."

Fausto pulled the sheet over his head, but as he did so one of the bags under his arm slipped off the bed. "Could you get that for me?"

Marcelino remained standing at the foot of the bed. "If you ever die," he said, "they're going to say you were a coward. They'll say you made it all up. You never went to Peru, you never led an army, you never explored the jungle, you never did what you said you did. They'll say you abandoned your men, you escaped . . . ."

"No!"

"Yes."

Fausto sat up and glared at his young friend. Who was he to throw out such insults? A shepherd . . . can't even find his way home. All he can do is play that flute.

"You're not even a good coward," Marcelino said. "A good coward would have died years ago. You shouldn't have even been born. Like my Uncle Celso used to say, life is a game for winners, not losers."

"What's that supposed to mean?"

"I don't know, but he used to say it."

Fausto flung his pillow at the bedpost. Marcelino ducked, but as he rose from his crouch, an ice-bag crashed into his chest and he collapsed on the floor.

"I'll show you who's a coward," Fausto said, lifting his bones from the bed. He nudged the figure on the floor. "Come on, we've got things to do."

"Just a moment . . . I . . . I can't breathe."

"Aha! Well, you can learn a few games yourself. Vamos."

Fausto adjusted the partial on the right side of his mouth, yanked his pith helmet down to his ears and strode out of the room. Stopping in the kitchen, he lifted the dishtowel covering the cage and poked a finger at the sleepy, arthritic bird. "Take care of the house, Tico. You're in charge now." The parakeet ruffled its feathers and seemed to shrug. Fausto gave him the remainder of the anis and said goodbye with a friendly tap on the back that left the bird sputtering by one claw above the water dish.

Crossing into the living room, Fausto heard his wife chuckle. "Aren't you forgetting something?" she said.

"Ah . . . yes."

Evangelina handed him the trousers. "I just ironed them. And here's your shirt. You might as well look neat."

Fausto steadied himself against the television while his wife lifted his leg. "Now the other side," she said, "that's it." She pulled up the zipper, careful not to pinch anything, then pushed the button through the hole. He expected her to say, "What would you do without me?" But this time Evangelina tied his cape, slowly, as if it were the last knot and simply said, "I'll be waiting for you."

Marcelino opened the door, and the two men stepped out. The Peruvian then handed Fausto the elegant, homemade scroll. He solemnly unrolled the parchment and began to read. "I, Don Fausto Tejada, respectful servant and emissary of Nuestra Ciudad la Reina de los Angeles, hereby undertake this journey, fitter for bodies less blasted with misfortune, for men of greater ability, so that if Your Grace wills it, I may be allowed to search this land . . . not in quest of riches but of the true seed and pulse of life . . . ."

No, he decided, it wouldn't do. It's one thing to enter the Valley of Mexico at the head of an army, or to lay my staff on the glory of Peru . . . but it's quite a different thing to be cast into the arms of a thousand starving men. The scroll would only make me look ridiculous. If I'm going to help them, I'll need more than words.

"Marcelino, play something," Fausto said as they turned the corner and started down the slope toward the river. "Anything . . . something that will help me think." Marcelino obliged, keeping the sound low so it wouldn't wake the neighbors.

". . . fitter for bodies less blasted with misfortune . . . ." Fausto shook his head. "It's too bad, it's not every day people can hear language like that. Well, maybe some other time . . . ."

The problem of the mojados called for something drastic, but Fausto had no idea where or how to find a solution. He recalled once before he had been in a similar situation. He was crossing the desert with a truckload of encyclopedias. Somewhere between Coachella and the Salton Sea the road stopped. He remembered he was so angry he jumped down and started kicking the sand where the road disappeared. Despite the noonday heat, he kept kicking the sand and cursing the men who had built such a disaster. After a while other trucks and cars arrived. The people saw what he was doing, and they began to do the same. By evening they had kicked sand all the way to Indio. But even then the problem still wasn't solved. Fausto had worn holes in the toes of his shoes, and the only shoestore open was sold out of his size.

No, he would have to think this out carefully. "Marcelino, that's enough music."

As they neared the levee, Fausto noticed the lights of Mrs. Rentería's house were on. They hurried across the street and took a closer look. The mojados, it seemed, had made themselves at home. Mrs. Rentería was serving them as fast as they could finish a plate and pass it on to the next hungry mouth. Apparently Smaldino had emptied his load of fish at the back door, and Tiburcio and his sons had made a barbecue pit using an old, chain-link fence stretched across the backyard over the sunken plot of pansies and geraniums. "I can always grow more flowers," Mrs. Rentería explained, "but these men only have one life to live." Fausto nodded and squeezed into the kitchen. Mrs. Noriega and several of the other women were busy kneading the dough and shaping it into football-size loaves. In the bathroom Cuca was whipping up enough eggs and milk to satisfy an army. And it was only when the foaming ponche rose over the bathtub did she realize she might have made more than enough.

Nothing that could be eaten was left in the house, nor in the houses for two blocks around. Filled and belching, the mojados wandered back to the river. Mrs. Rentería almost offered them her heart but then changed her mind when she remembered someone would have to give them breakfast.

"Fausto," she said, "don't you think they should be inside? If only I had more room in the house. But you saw how it was. I could hardly move."

"How about the church," Mrs. Noriega suggested, moving her rosary hand up a bead. "I've been praying all night for God to help us."

"That won't do no good," Tiburcio said. "All they can do in a church is pray. No, señora, they didn't come all the way from Mexico to pray."

"At least they won't be cold."

Tiburcio looked at Fausto. "What were *you* going to do with them? You're the one that brought them here."

"I had an idea, but now I don't know .... I don't think they want to die."

"Well, we've got to put them somewhere, or they'll be arrested. I know, it's happened to me."

"Mario!" Fausto shouted, startling the women who were dozing in chairs by the kitchen table.

Mario pushed himself up from the bathtub. He had been rinsing the ring of ponche from around the top.

"Mario, tell them to come back. We'll take them to the theater."

"What theater?"

"The Los Feliz theater, the one they closed last year. Can you open it?"

"Sure, but what you gonna do when you get 'em in? I know them vatos. They're gonna want a movie."

"I'll worry about that. Just do what I said."

"What'll I tell 'em?"

"Say they're going to a show."

"What's it called? They're gonna ask what's it called."

"I don't know, make something up."

"Vida y muerte?" Tiburcio suggested.

"No," Mrs. Rentería said, "that's too depressing. You need something that will make them happy . . . ."

"I know," Mrs. Noriega said, "la vida de Jesús."

No one answered, then Tiburcio said the title should have some mystery to it, maybe something about a man with a mask.

"No, what you need is something with a woman," Mario said.

"Yeah, who's going to play the woman?"

"You mean, we gotta put the thing on?"

"Sure, it's easy, just think of something."

Cuca suggested a show about Burma.

"Where's that?" someone asked.

"Next to India."

"Why not Los Angeles?"

"Hollywood . . . ."

"Glendale."

"¡Qué Glendale! ¡Maravilla!"

"Boyle Heights . . . ."

"The Paladium."

"The zoo . . . ."

Later, as the mojados began to pass by, Fausto winked to Marcelino and shouldered his way through the crowd of excited neighbors.

"They'll follow us in a little while," he said. "Once they start talking like that, it's no use staying. No one listens anyway."

ELEVEN

The show was more than Fausto had dreamed was possible. Popcorn, pirulís and candied apples were passed along the rows, from aisle to aisle; somehow the lights were made to work, and the children quickly cleaned off the stage by skating back and forth on pieces of gunny sacks. Fausto sat in the second row. He signaled for Mario to draw the curtains back — waterstained and torn at the bottom — then motioned to Marcelino to play an opening tune. For a moment the mojados were silent, waiting for something called "The Road to Tamazunchale." One boy, seated three seats from Fausto, was especially quiet. His hometown was Tamazunchale, and he had never heard of a show with such a name. The Río Moctezuma, which came down from the town of Terrazas, had figured in a movie he once saw, and he even recognized a hill near his house — but never, he had never seen a show all about the place that had given him birth. It was a great honor, something he would tell his mother and father.

After some difficulty with the guide ropes, the curtains parted and Tiburcio emerged from a cloud of snow. Or smog, no one could tell. He was dressed in a black suit, and the white collar of his stiff, studded shirt was turned up so that the plastic stays jabbed into his jowls, giving his face the appearance of a retired circus master.

"Psst, your collar," his wife called from the band pit.

"Hermanos," he said in a loud voice, ignoring his wife and stepping to the edge of the stage, "we have called the show you are about to see Tamazunchale . . . ."

"Psst! The road . . . ."

"Yes, the road to Tamazunchale . . . for a very special reason. You see, whenever things go bad, whenever we don't like someone, whoever it is . . . our sons, our wife, our compadres or comadres . . . we simply send them to Tamazunchale. We've never really seen this place, but it sounds better than saying the other, if you know what I mean. Uh, before I go any further, is there anyone here from Tamazunchale?"

The boy in the second row swallowed and dropped his hand into the popcorn.

"Good," Tiburcio said. "Otherwise, we would have to change the name of our show . . . to Teocaltiche . . . Panindícuaro or something like that."

He waited for the whistling and laughter to die, then continued.

Under his wife's coaching, he rambled to the end of his speech, explaining to his audience how they were all either coming from or going to Tamazunchale. "And we are too," he added. "We may not know it, but it's the same road. Everyone is on that road. Sí, compadres, everyone! But as you'll see, Tamazunchale is not what you think it is . . . ."

"Psst, hurry up."

"Lady," Tiburcio said, nodding to his wife, "and gentlemen . . . our show!"

Tiburcio retreated to a burst of applause. The footlights clicked on, and someone, probably Robert, Smaldino's eldest son, hobbled out from the side, a hoe in one hand and wearing a shabby pith helmet, a moth-eaten cape and baggy trousers. Black, crayon wrinkles were drawn above and below his eyes and at both sides of his mouth. As he came into the light, a small girl in pigtails skipped by, then returned with a puzzled expression.

"Tío," she said, "where are you going?"

"Tamazunchale," the old man replied.

"Can I go too?"

"No, mijita. I only have one ticket."

"I've got eleven cents."

The old man touched the girl's cheek with his palm. "Well, maybe they'll let you go free."

"Can I bring my frog?"

"Of course, I know they don't sell frog tickets."

As soon as they were seated on the bus, the driver began collecting tickets. The old man handed him his.

"One more," the driver said, "the little girl . . . ."

"Can she ride on my lap? She won't bother."

The man glanced at the other passengers. "Alright, but the frog stays."

One more passenger was let on, a woman with a neat pompadour wave, a shoulder-padded suit and white gloves. Fausto stood from his second-row seat in the audience and shouted his wife's name.

"Sit down!"

"I can't see . . . ."

"Shut up, I can't hear."

Carmela, acting as usherette, hurried down the aisle, waving her flashlight, and asked her uncle to sit and be quiet.

When the bags, suitcases, boxes and paper sacks were tucked under the seats or onto the overhead racks, the bus began to shake

103

itself of the cold, gnashing its gears, finally lumbering onto the main road to Tamazunchale. On the bumper were the words EL DIABLO NEGRO.

For a while the passengers appeared content to gaze through the windows, flip through magazines, stare ahead or simply close their eyes. Eventually the heat of the engine rose into the seats of those in the rear, the sunlight burned through the roof, and the familiar odor of gassy meals was loosed on the people toward the front. Evangelina, already squirming, was the first to complain. Gripping the seat rail with both gloved hands, she rose and demanded that the driver control his passengers. When he ignored her pleas, she asked to be let off. Fausto couldn't blame her, for even he could smell the bomb, seated where he was in the audience.

The woman stepped down and pointed a white finger at the flashy uniform and shiny-billed cap. "You're the one, you did it!"

"So? It's my bus."

The audience laughed, and as the bus lurched forward, a bag bulging with fish toppled from the overhead rack. A young woman cradling a baby shrieked at the shower of scaly things dropping down her back, under her bodice and into her hair. Ignoring his mother's hysterics, the baby quietly began sucking on the head of a mackerel.

Smaldino, dressed as Smaldino, apologized his way to the front of the bus and was ordered to leave. Someone heaved a fish at him, but it hit the driver. Smaldino grinned and jumped to the ground.

Jess was the next passenger to leave the bus, but it wasn't because he wanted to. While he was rereading his only copy of *Mechanics Illustrated*, Cuca, the director of the show, motioned from behind the curtain for everyone to leave. It was a rest stop, and they were supposed to act like tired, stretching, yawning, hungry passengers. Jess refused.

"Get him off the stage," Cuca whispered to the driver. "He's ruining everything."

The driver pushed his cap back and approached the lone figure on the bus. "Get off."

"Why?" Jess asked, keeping his finger on the page.

"Don't ask," the driver said in Jess's ear.

"Hey, I thought I was just going to sit."

"Shhh! Get off."

"No, I'm reading."

The driver grabbed him by the arm, but Jess, remembering his wrestling holds, jabbed the man in the ribs, feinted and tried to trip him off his feet. The mojados seemed to like what they saw — two men fighting like stags, head to head, then like bears, chest to chest, finally like men, wheeling all over the stage and flailing at each other like wild animals. On the bus the neat rows of foldup chairs folded and fell, the mock sides of the roof caved in, the egg-crate engine died, and the bamboo steering wheel collapsed. With the help of the other male passengers, the wrestling champ was dethroned and carried into the alley behind the theater. While everyone in the audience was laughing, Mario pulled the curtains together, and the props were set up again. So far the show was a success.

The second scene was more of the first. Mrs. Rentería, playing Mrs. Rentería, had to leave when her companion died. The passengers offered their sympathy, and the driver even covered the dead man's face with his own jacket.

"Thank you," the spinster said, "he'll need something to keep him warm."

"Don't mention it."

"You wouldn't have another pair of pants, would you? His are wet."

"These are all I've got, and I can't drive without them."

"Please?"

"I'm sorry, I can't."

Mrs. Rentería started to cry, the dead man moaned under the jacket, and someone in the audience shouted for the driver to hand over his pants. Soon the men were all chanting, "Pan-ta-lones! Pan-ta-lones!"

The driver turned his back to the passengers, removed his wallet, comb, coins and nailclipper from the pockets, then unbuckled the pants and slipped them off. As he handed them over, the children on the stage giggled.

"Thank you," Mrs. Rentería said, and everyone applauded the man's generosity.

Not long afterward, the bus on its way again, Mrs. Noriega announced she was leaving. They had gone far enough, and she would walk the rest of the way. "Only God knows if we lie," she said, facing the others. "He knows when people lie. I promised him I would walk, and a promise to God is the most sacred promise of all. It is more sacred than the promises we make to the saints, and yes, even more sacred, more serious than the promises we make to our holy mother in heaven. How many of you have made promises, how many of you can swear . . . ."

"Señora," the driver said, "I promised to drive the bus to Tamazunchale. We're behind schedule as it is. Could you . . .?"

"God bless you all," Mrs. Noriega said. "In the name of the Father, the Son and the Holy Ghost . . . ."

One by one, as the road neared its end, the passengers left the bus. A woman with five children thought she recognized her home and asked to be let off. Two drunks in the rear fell off their chairs and were left with their faces in the dust. Another man, swearing his ancestors had created the sun, remained in the desert to discover the truth. Everyone had their reasons. Even the driver, as they came into view of the town, stopped the bus and said he could go no further.

The old man with the little girl complained. They were the only passengers left, and he was determined to see this place everyone talked about. "Are you coming back?" he shouted as the young man hopped down and darted into the field of maguey plants.

"You can walk the rest of the way. I can't drive into that town without my pants. I'm sorry, but everybody knows who I am."

The old man shrugged and pushed up on his staff. "Vámonos, mijita, it's getting late."

Cuca told Mario to lower the lights, and the twilight of Tamazunchale instantly descended. Then the curtains closed, and the audience was silent, uncertain if the show was over.

Backstage, the chairs were removed, and Tiburcio and his sons quickly propped up the set for the last scene. Between two arched, cardboard trees, bending toward the middle, they placed a plywood ramp leading up to the sky. One of the smaller boys climbed up a ladder and scissor-locked his legs around a rafter. Then he dangled a small white cloud from a string.

"Ready?" Cuca asked, waiting for the cloud to stop moving.

"Yeah," the boy said.

The old man and the girl took their positions at the front of the stage, and the curtains were swept back. Something near the ceiling snapped, and Mario was left with the rope in his hands.

"Shh, quiet!" Cuca said, stamping her foot.

"Tío," the girl started, straining her eyes over the unwadded sheet of paper, "I'm afraid."

"Don't worry, we're almost there."

The two figures walked in circles for a while, then the girl tugged at her uncle's cape again. "Why are we going to this place?"

The old man sat down at the bottom of the ramp. "To see what it's like."

"Is it a bad place?"

"Who said that?"

"There's a boy who sits next to me in school, and he's always

106

using that word. The other day the teacher heard him, and he had to stand in the corner for an hour. The teacher really got mad because he even wrote it on the wall. But that's nothing, I see it in the bathroom all the time."

"You think your teacher is right?"

"I don't know, she says we should wash our mouth out with soap if we ever say it. But once I heard her say it to another teacher. I watched her for a long time, and she never washed her mouth."

"Don't you think it's silly to wash your mouth with soap?"

"Yeah, toothpaste is better."

"Mijita . . . everyone should go to Tamazunchale."

"What's it like?"

"Like any other place. Oh, a few things are different . . . if you want them to be."

"What do you mean?"

"Well, if you see a bird, you can talk to it, and it'll talk back. If you want something, it's yours. If you want to be an apple, think about it and you might be hanging from a tree or you might be held in someone's hand, maybe your own."

"Could I be a flower?"

"You can be the sun."

"How 'bout the moon?"

"You can be the stars . . . ."

"What if I want to be me again?"

"Mijita, you can be a song of a million sounds, or you can be a little girl listening to one sound."

"Tío, you think I'll see my friends?"

"All of them."

"Lucy and Sally? They're my best friends."

"Lucy and Sally."

"Will they have to go home?"

"Not unless their mother calls them."

"How long will we stay?"

"As long as you want . . . forever . . . it doesn't matter to me."

The little girl sneaked a look at the cloud in the sky. "Tío, are we going to die?"

"No one dies in Tamazunchale."

"No one?"

"Well, some people do, but they're only pretending."

"Like in the movies?"

"Not exactly. They do die, they're even buried and people cry, and some of the men become very drunk . . . ."

"Like Tiburcio?"

"Sí, mijita."

"Then what happens to the dead people?"

"They usually see how stupid it is to die, so they come out of the earth and do something else."

"Do we have to die if we don't want to?"

"Not unless you're curious. That's what happens to most people. They have to try it once. But don't worry about that now. You'll have lots of time to think about it later."

The old man wiped his brow and tucked the script under his cape. He glanced down at the frightened little eyes. "Don't be afraid, we're almost there."

"Tío, why didn't we stay home like my Tía Eva said?"

"Because Tamazunchale *is* our home. Once we're there, we're free, we can be everything and everyone. If you want, you can even be nothing."

"Will I have to go to school?"

"Never."

"Okay."

The old man stood and faced the sky. "Shall we go?"

"Tío, what about the snow? Yesterday you said you'd take me to the mountains to see the snow."

"Mijita, you can be a snowball."

"Really?"

"I'll make you myself."

The little girl laughed and skipped up the ramp.

"Wait," the old man said, pivoting around his staff and gesturing to the audience. "Excuse me, but maybe you would like to come with us . . .?"

The first one up on the stage was the Tamazunchale boy; he could clearly see his hometown at the top of the ramp. A few others followed him, then more, and in minutes the theater seats were empty. The column, led by the old man and the girl, quickly formed and wound up into the sky. Fausto could see that gradually some of the mojados were dipping to the right or to the left, but most continued forward, and eventually all were lost, diminished, gone between the horizon and the stars.

Alone in the second row of the theater, Fausto clapped and clapped until his hands were sore.

TWELVE

"Why is he clapping his hands?"

"Looks like he's having a seizure."

"Don't say that! You think he's crazy or something?"

"I didn't say that. I just said he looks like fever's got him. You ever seen anybody shake like that?"

"I did."

"What are you, a doctor?"

"No, but I saw a guy shaking like that. Only worse. And he didn't clap his hands."

"Shh! Keep it down."

"Hey, man . . . ."

"Don't call me man."

"Alright, esa . . . ."

"Stop it! You think you're a pachuco or something?"

"Relax . . . ."

"What about the guy you saw? What happened to him?"

"Yeah, that's all I was gonna say. Let 'im tell us what it was."

"Maybe we should go downstairs. What if he hears us?"

"He's okay, probably like a good story."

"That's it, he's dying, and you men tell stories."

"What else can we do?"

"Pray for him . . . ."

"I already called the doctor."

"What did he say?"

"Not much. He says the coughing's probably from emphesyma, he can't move because of his heart, and the fever might be from a cold."

"Hey, what about the vato with the shakes?"

"Isn't he coming?"

"He's dead."

"No, the doctor."

"He said he'll be right over as soon as he can get away."

"Pinche doctors, that's what happened to my old man. The ambulance wouldn't even take him."

"Lower your voice."

"What for? It's the truth."

"You'll wake him up. I think he's sleeping now, he's not clapping his hands anymore."

"You should all be praying. I suppose nobody called the priest."

"Could you, señora? I forgot."

"I thought so."

"Tell him to hurry."

"You, all of you can pray, that's what you can do."

"Sí, señora."

"Pray for his soul."

"Sí, señora . . . ."

"Now tell us the story."

"It was my buddy in Okinawa. We were hiding in a cave. You know, over there they bury their dead in caves."

"What were you doing there?"

"Do you have to talk so loud? You'll wake him up."

"Let 'im finish."

"They put them in these caves, then they put these big bottles of sake . . . ."

"What's that?"

"I thought you weren't listening?"

"Leave her alone. Sake's wine, they make it out of rice. It's supposed to help the dead on their way to heaven."

"So what happened?"

"We climbed into this cave, me and Bagus . . . ."

"Bagus?"

"That was his name, Charlie Bagus. He said lots of people in his town had names like that. I was always with the other Mexicans in the platoon, but I don't know, we were being hit pretty hard and somehow I got stuck with Bagus. But he was a nice guy, always kept his hair combed, even under his helmet. Only way you could get him mad was to mess up his hair."

"What about the cave?"

"Oh, so we were hiding in this cave. For four days we stayed in there, waiting for our guys to come and get us. Only thing that kept us alive was all that sake. But the third day I got bit by a scorpion. I thought I'd die. Bit me right on my . . . tú sabes, right here."

"What were you doing, digging holes with it?"

"I was pissing on the dead. Yeah, you'll do anything when you're drunk."

"Sounds perverted."

"Hey, watch your uncle."

"Anything's possible in a war."

"Still sounds perverted."

"So there I am, crying about my bite. The whole thing got big as my arm."

"Wow!"

"Heavy, man."

"But that wasn't nothing compared to Bagus. I think some mosquito bit him, 'cause he got the shakes like I've never seen. All I could do was rub him down with sake. When the place was cleared and I dragged him out, they had to take him away in a strait jacket. Later they told me he died."

"That's gross."

"Well, people do die."

"I mean you pissing on the bodies."

"Just bones. What do they know?"

"Yeah, what's a bunch of bones?"

"I'll tell you another story, better than that one."

"Talk downstairs." Carmela wiped her uncle's brow and asked Mario to wet another washcloth with cold water. Smaldino pulled Tiburcio aside and asked about the other story, which was also about the war and him being the only survivor of a landing craft that was bombed before they hit the shore. Tiburcio had saved himself because he was the first one off.

"Shhhh!"

"What can you say? You turn around, and the whole boat's blown to hell."

"Shhhhhhhhh!"

When the new priest arrived, Carmela asked him what happened to the regular priest.

"I'm the substitute," the young man said. "Father Jaime's ill. By the way, would all of you mind leaving for a few minutes? I'd like to be alone for the absolution."

"Mind if I stay?" Mario asked.

"Are you immediate family?"

"His son."

"His son? I wasn't told he had a son. The lady who brought me here said he only had a niece."

"Then why'd you ask? I bet you like to see people lie."

"This is no time to argue. Please, move over by the door."

"What if I don't?"

"Mario! Leave the father alone."

"Miss, will you please ask him to move?"

"Mario, let's go."

"No, I'm stayin' right here, just like your Tío would want me to. Ain't that right, Mister Fausto?"

Fausto slowly raised his lids and winked with his good eye.

111

"See, what d'I tell you?"

"Okay . . . but please move out of the light."

"What for?"

"Mario, stay back like he says."

"En nomine, patri——"

"Don't gimme none of that mambo zambo shit. I wanna know what you're sayin'."

"Miss, can you please control him?"

"Hey, you know what, ese? I bet you don't believe all that stuff. Right?"

The priest continued, trying to ignore the youthful shadow blocking the light.

"You're all the same," Mario said. "They did that to my dad . . . and what good did it do him? Nothin'. He still died . . . ."

Carmela coaxed Mario into the hallway and told him the priest was here to give her uncle the last rites. "He's not going to save him. He's praying for his soul."

"Soul, shit! That's just a word. Man . . . I mean, Carmela . . . what would you do if there wasn't no such thing? What would you do?"

"I don't think anybody knows if there is or there isn't. Nobody really knows."

"I mean, let's say you knew. Let's say God told you."

"Don't be silly."

"I mean what if he came down on his horse and . . . ."

"His horse?"

"Then his cow, I don't care. What if he stood right here and said hi, it's me, the big chingón, and I'm tellin' you all this soul stuff is a pile of caca. What would you do?"

"Mario, go downstairs. I don't think you're funny."

"I'm not being funny. I'm just askin' you a simple question. What would you do?"

"I don't know . . . think about it I suppose, maybe ask my tío."

"Right! And you know what he'd say? He'd say God was right."

"How do you know?"

"He told me."

"My tío or God?"

"Him, your uncle, the old man lyin' on the bed in there. See, that's why I was givin' the padrecito a hard time. If he knew what your uncle was thinkin', he wouldn't be givin' him no lost rite."

"Last."

"Hey, you know what I mean."

When the priest finished, Fausto again opened his eyes, smiled and gave the young man a blessing of his own.

"Thank you, Father," Carmela said in the hallway. She followed him downstairs and walked him to the door.

"He's a strange man," the priest said. "I had this feeling he could have confessed, but maybe I'm wrong."

"No, you're probably right. He likes to play games."

"That's a serious game."

"I know, Father . . . his soul and all that."

"All that? There's nothing more serious than the salvation of the soul."

"I'll tell him, Father."

As the priest was leaving, Doctor Ramírez arrived, followed by Cuca with her bag of medicines.

"He's upstairs in bed, doctor."

"Fine, this won't take long."

"Cuca, would you mind waiting until he's through?"

"No, I've got all day. Besides, first come, first serve."

"Thanks."

"Carmela, do you have anything to eat? I'm hungry."

"Sure, if those two in the kitchen haven't finished what there is. Check over the refrigerator, there should be a box of graham crackers. Oh, and can you give one to the bird? I'll be up with the doctor."

Doctor Ramírez was briefer than the priest. He poked a thermometer under Fausto's tongue, took his blood pressure, then listened to his heart and lungs.

"Want me to call the hearst?" Mario asked.

"That won't be necessary, and please, lower your voice."

"It don't bother him."

"It bothers *me.*" The doctor read the temperature and nodded.

"Isn't there something you can do?" Carmela asked.

"I'll write you a prescription. Give him one every half hour."

"Hey, doc, I think he's tellin' you somethin'."

Doctor Ramírez turned and saw the bony finger wagging a feeble no above the blanket.

"Do as you wish," the doctor said, closing his bag. "Here's the prescription, and call if you want me to certify cause of death."

"Thank you, doctor."

"Thank you shit! You ain't done nothin'."

"Who's he?"

"A friend of my uncle's."

"A friend?"

"Yeah, don't I look like a friend?"

"Yes, yes . . . as I said, just call if you need me."

"Puto."

"Mario! Control yourself . . . . Doctor, I'll go down with you."

"I can manage. You better stay with the boy. I think he's upset."

In the kitchen Cuca was making a ponche in the blender for Tiburcio and Smaldino. She had been telling them about her years as a midwife in the Chihuahua sierra. Whenever Cuca loosened up, no one, except maybe Fausto, could tell a better story. She had just finished describing the birth of what everyone was certain would be the devil himself. But the baby was unimportant, Cuca said, the little girl was normal. What was strange were the parents. The mother had some sort of leprosy and kept her nose, ears and parts of her fingers in little glass jars, and her most private part she managed to save in an envelope. As for the father, he looked retarded, but he wasn't. People made him that way. He crawled around outside his hut digging up roots and stealing chickens from the houses down below in the valley. The people had already cut off one hand when he was a child, but that didn't stop his stealing. He said he worked with the devil, and everyone would run whenever they saw this man crawling into the town.

"Aren't you afraid they'll cut off your other hand, I asked him. He laughed and held up a devil's suit he made out of a tablecloth and some stolen rags. Then he said if I ever told anyone, he'd put on his real suit and come down to get me."

"Did you ever tell?" Tiburcio asked.

"That night, I think, because I left the next day."

"What happened?"

"Nothing."

"They didn't catch him?"

"They knew all along. They said they felt sorry for him and his wife. And what's a few chickens? Everyone has a right to a few chickens."

Cuca's next story was about another town. A woman was dying in childbirth.

"Cuca!" Carmela called from the top of the stairs, "the doctor's gone. You can come up now."

"I'll be there, let me finish this first."

"Please, the doctor said he's . . . ."

"Carmela, he's waited this long, he can wait until I finish my story."

"Hurry, please!"

The baby was born, Cuca said, and the mother lived. But the little creature was a hermaphrodite.

"What's that?" Smaldino asked.

"Boy and girl."

"Twins?"

"No," Tiburcio said, describing with his hands. "She means it had a girl part . . . and a boy part."

"Oh."

Cuca placed the blender with the ponche on the table and continued. The father became so angry after he saw his child that he demanded she make it a boy. "Sew it up, he said. Do something, but make it a boy."

"You can't do that," Smaldino said.

"Yeah," Tiburcio added, "how could you be sure which thing was the one it used?"

"I don't think you can tell," Cuca said. "But this man had a rifle at my back, and I'm sure he would have used it if I didn't think of something."

"Cuca!" Carmela shouted again, "I think my tío wants to see you."

"Alright, I'm coming."

"So what did you do?" Tiburcio asked.

"Guess."

"I don't know."

"Me neither. All I know about is fish, and who cares about them."

Cuca said she told the father he was right, it was a boy.

"How could you tell?"

"I couldn't, now let me finish . . . . I told the man he had two choices. He could cut off the boy's penis or ignore the vagina. No! he said, I could never do that to my own son."

"Me neither."

"So I told him he could wait until the boy was old enough to understand, then explained to him that some people are born with two things and some are born with three."

Smaldino swallowed. "Three?"

"Your asshole," Tiburcio said.

"Oh, yeah . . . ."

"Who would look at the boy anyway, I told him. The only people that knew were him, his wife and me. And I was leaving."

"What if the boy wanted to get married?"

"So? It's not impossible."

"And what if he turned out a girl?"

"You know, that's the trouble with you two. You don't look at the good side. Imagine how much fun it would be."

"I don't know," Tiburcio said.

"Yeah, I'll stick to my fish."

"Now," Cuca said, moving into the living room, "let's see what I can do for Fausto."

"Cuca."

"What?"

"Your bag."

"No, I won't need it."

Fausto clapped his hands twice as she entered. His eyes were closed, so she knew he was either joking or dreaming.

Carmela stood beside her. "Can you do something?"

"I didn't come to cure him. All I can do is talk to him and be here when he dies."

"She's right," Mario said. "She's not a magician."

"I just thought . . . oh, never mind."

"Stay," Cuca said. "He knows we're here."

Tiburcio and Smaldino entered the room with a pineapple-upside-down cake and a bag of avocados. Mrs. Rentería had left them for Fausto . . . "in case he was hungry."

"Leave it in the kitchen," Carmela said.

"All right if we eat some of the cake?" Smaldino asked.

"Sure."

"Save some for me," Mario said.

Tiburcio stared for a moment at his dying friend, then moved the cake beneath the scrawny nose. "Just want to let him smell it. It's his favorite."

"Why don't we play a little music," Smaldino suggested. "He always liked music."

The record player was brought in, along with several of Fausto's old 78's. A few more chairs were placed in the room, and the cake was cut. Jess, on his lunchbreak, had just walked in and was handed ten dollars.

"Buy something to drink," Carmela said.

He wiped his hands on the grease-stained overalls and took the money.

"Hey," Mario said, "let me buy it. I'll get double what he gets."

"No, you stay here."

"Trust me."

"Mario, we have enough problems without you bringing the police."

"One time? I promise nothin'll happen."

"Okay, give him the money."

After the mariachis started, Jess examined the gray face on the bed, then nudged Carmela with an elbow. "Did he write a will?"

"What for?"

"The house, furniture . . . ."

"And the bird. Jess, not now."

"Well, did he?"

"He was writing something last night."

"Where is it?"

"Over there, on the dresser."

Jess opened the scroll and read the words with his lips.

"What's it say?"

"I don't know, it's got a lot of big words . . ."

"Spanish?"

"I don't know, it looks foreign."

"Forget it, Jess. It doesn't really matter."

Mario returned with a fifth of bourbon, a pint of Strawberry Hill and two six-packs of Coors. "Hey, people, here it is!"

Tiburcio and Smaldino went for the beer, Cuca asked for wine, Carmela said she'd try a little bourbon — "with rocks" — Jess said he would wait, and Mario insisted he would share some anís with Fausto.

"He can't drink," Carmela said.

"Wait'll you see this," Mario said, uncapping a small bottle he had hidden in his coat pocket. "He ain't dead yet."

"Mario, don't!"

Again, ever so slightly, Fausto wagged his index finger at his niece. Then slowly the tip of his thirsty, quivering tongue appeared between his lips.

The song from the stereo had ended, and Carmela stepped across the room to turn the record over.

"Wait," Mario said. "Hear that?"

"What?"

"That music, hear it?"

"I don't hear nothing," Jess said.

"Listen."

Cuca bowed her head and tried to listen to every possible sound. Carmela cupped a hand to one ear, and the two beer drinkers said they couldn't hear anything.

"That's his friend," Mario said, "the vato with the flute."

Jess raised the window and searched the scummy haze hanging over the levee and the freightyards. "It's the trains," he said, "them squeaking trains."

No one spoke, and after a while the stereo set was closed and put away.

"Go answer the door," Cuca said. "I think someone's outside."

"Come on in!" Carmela called out the window. "The door's open."

Tiburcio drained his beer can. "Probably my wife. She said she'd be over as soon as her hair was dry."

"Have another beer," Mario said.

"No, I've had enough."

"Carmela, more bourbon?"

"No thanks, I don't feel too good."

"Señora, more wine . . .?"

Cuca, seated by the bed, was silent. She wiped the dribble from Fausto's mouth, and for a long time listened to the brittle wheeze coming from his withered throat, stared at the sallow, sagging face, at the thin, crooked fingers, and waited for one more clap.

THIRTEEN

There was no funeral, no burial. Instead, Fausto insisted they take him to the beach so he could look at the sea and the women in bikinis for a while. Evangelina, as a last gesture, had promised he could do anything as long as it wasn't indecent. When he had filled his mind with enough bodies to last several lifetimes, he left the umbrella and said he wanted to go to a bookstore.

"What you wanna do there?" Mario asked.

"Where I'm going, nobody sells books. Maybe I can open a little shop."

Fausto purchased more books than they could carry. Diaries, journals, crates of paperbacks, encyclopedias in five languages, a Nahua grammar, a set of Chinese classics, a few novels by a promising Bulgarian author, a collection of Japanese prints, an illustrated Time-Life series on nature, an early cosmography of the known and unknown worlds, a treatise on the future of civilization in the Sea of Cortez, two coffee-table editions on native American foods, an anthology of uninvented myths and three boxes of unwritten books.

"But Tío, look, nothing's in them. It's all blank pages. Why don't you take some books from over there. I saw some real nice ones."

"No, I want these."

"What for?"

"Some people might want to write their own books. If I'm going to own a store, I want to have everything."

Fausto had toddled up and down the aisles, choosing by color, shape, size, cover, sometimes by title. At the sale table he even wormed his arm down to the bottom of the pile and fished up a neglected, indexed history of historiography. Then everything was taken to the front of the store.

"Now what?" Carmela asked him at the cashier's counter.

The automatic doors parted and Mario, followed by Marcelino, pushed in a train of shopping carts they had borrowed from the A&P down the block. While everyone was stacking books into the carts, Tiburcio and Smaldino strayed over to another counter and slowly flipped their way through an illustrated sex manual.

Tiburcio's wife threw a wine-taster's guide at the two men. "Come on, you guys, help!"

"Let them look," Fausto said. "They're only pictures, ¿que no?"

119

"It's pictures like that that give me babies. You know, sometimes I wish he were blind."

"What would that do? He's still got pictures in his head."

"I don't care if they're in his toes, he doesn't have to look."

When the carts were ready, Mario began whispering to the young clerk behind the counter. She was smiling.

"What's he doing?" Carmela asked her uncle.

"Watch."

It wasn't long before Mario's suggestions had transformed the ponytailed brunette into a giant pink chrysanthemum. Her petals unfolded with a slow-motion grace that left everyone with their mouths open.

Mrs. Rentería was the first to approach. "I'd love to pick her," she said.

"I don't think she'd like that," Fausto cautioned. "You see, that's why she wants to be a flower. If you took her home, you'd be the only one to see her."

"I'll take her by the roots and plant her in the front yard. I'll be careful."

"No, that's stealing . . . or kidnapping."

"Then let Mario take her out."

Everyone looked at Mario, still with his goatee but now wearing tennis shorts and a see-through velveteen shirt. "Not me," he said, "I'm a weightlifter. No more stealin' for me." He hoisted three boxes of books and trundled another cartload out to the line of parked cars. When he returned, he walked with his legs spread apart, as if he suffered from piles, and his head and rippling giant's neck seemed to grow out of a mountainous wall of chest. "Ain't nobody going to mess with me now," he told Fausto, "not even that vato with the dog. Hey, why don't we go up to the park and look for him?"

"Later," Fausto said, "first let's get all my books."

For a while Mario lumbered around Tiburcio and Smaldino, flexing and lifting tables and bookshelves. Finally he lifted the two men high into the air. They lost their place in the book, but otherwise they hardly seemed to notice. Mrs. Noriega gasped, and several customers hid behind the science fiction display.

"Don't worry," Fausto said, "he won't hurt them. Mario! Finish taking out the books."

Mrs. Rentería stroked the chrysanthemum. "Fausto, aren't you stealing the books?"

"Señora, I'm not a thief. As soon as I sell them, I'll give the money to the store."

"Then I'll buy my flower. Here's fifty cents. Should I leave it on the counter?"

"You realize you're taking a person. That flower is a person. Don't you see how she's watching us? She knows. And I think she'll be very sad if you take her away from her family, her work, maybe even the one she loves."

"Yes, you're right. I never thought about it that way."

Outside on the sidewalk a crowd had gathered around Hercules. He was lifting volunteers over his head. Behind the crowd Cuca and Mrs. Noriega's grandchildren were plying the parking meters with dimes.

"Tío, don't look now, but I think that flower girl's changing."

"Mario stole her show . . . . Well, we've got everything. Let's go."

Fausto and his neighbors hurried into the cars.

"Don't go!" Tiburcio's wife shouted. "They're still in the store."

Fausto rolled down the window of Carmela's '47 Plymouth and called out to Marcelino, who was already comfortably reclined on the roof. "Go get them, and use your flute if you have to."

The shepherd dropped down the sloping trunk and ran into the store. In a moment he returned between the automatic doors. Under each arm he held a large illustrated book.

"What do I do with them?"

"Give them to their wives."

The books were given to the women, and Marcelino, gathering his poncho, leaped onto the car again. For the time being Tiburcio lay pressed under the weight of an expansive, fleshy seat, while Smaldino, offering himself as a treasure, pleasantly lost himself in his wife's mind.

The procession followed the Santa Monica Freeway as far as Vermont, then wound through downtown Los Angeles, past Bullocks, Clifton's, the Million Dollar Theater, skirting the old mission, Calle Olvera, and finally along North Broadway, over the river and tracks, crossing Daly and stopping at the Cuatro Milpas take-out and restaurant. Not one car had been lost, they were all together. And hungry. This time Fausto remained in the car, while Carmela and most of the adults left to bring the food.

"Tío, what do you want?"

"A number four, with a gordita. And get an empanada for Tico."

"You want milk?"

"Get me a beer. Carta Blanca if they have it."

Fausto teased the parakeet with his finger. Suddenly Tico-Tico raised his furry head from the old man's shirt pocket and without a word climbed out as a fully grown Siamese cat.

Fausto winced and rubbed the scratches on his chest. "Tico! Look what you did. My pocket's ripped." He ordered cat to sit above the seat, out of the way. "Be good and I'll give you a gordita."

The food was brought out in paper plates covered with aluminum foil, the drinks in paper bags. Fausto told everyone to follow Carmela's car to Elysian Park where they could picnic on tables and the children would have someplace to play. "And hurry, or someone might turn into something else." He glanced at Tiburcio, who apparently had been squeezed of all courage and had returned to being a husband. But Smaldino wouldn't think of changing. His wife was still excited by the new possibilities for their middle-age love. She held him close to her breasts and every now and then, when her children weren't looking, took a peek at a different page.

By the time they arrived at the park Mrs. Noriega had shrunken to a string of beads with a tiny silver cross dangling from her mouth. During the ride the rosary had slipped off the loose foil, settling between the beans and the enchiladas.

Except for the cars, the park was deserted. The streets were gone, some trees had shriveled, others had grown. Squirrels poked their heads out of the leaves on the ground, a bank of snow lay gleaming on the ridge below the blue, richly blue sky. A fantailed pigeon escaped the jaws of a snake by swooping up as a hawk, losing itself among the uppermost pines. And there was silence, then the sounds of other birds, of crickets, of frogs by the eddies of a stream. A rabbit moved among the ferns, a twig cracked under the weight of age and a bobcat's paw. The grasses grew high, and the flowers bent with the breeze, then sprang back and curled their heads to the sun. The scent of pine and sage mingled with the smells of moist earth, tiny onion shoots and the tangled fountains of wild strawberries.

Fausto, Carmela and the others forgot their food and descended to the ground. And as they did so, the cars shook themselves from bumper to bumper and galloped across the stream and into the trees. The old man sat on a broken tree limb and watched them all roll in the grass. Suddenly a green grasshopper latched onto his nose.

"Señora," Fausto softly warned, "be careful of the spiders."

Mrs. Noriega briefly wiggled her abdomen and leaped into the air.

In the distance Cuca trotted around like a fox, sniffing, poking, tasting every usable herb and plant, from pole to pole, from arctic ferns and alpine reeds to the mosses of Tierra del Fuego. For a long time Fausto watched the changes of his neighbors, the quirky cartwheels of minds in flight. Now a stork, now a bear, one minute a horse, the next minute the rider, one moment a dog's howl, the next moment the rustle of wind through the highest trees. It was all a game, free and forever.

But he himself, sitting above them all, would not change. He was too tired.

"And you didn't take your pills," Evangelina said from behind. "But I suppose it's too late for that now."

Without turning, Fausto patted the space beside him and gestured for her to sit down. Evangelina sat, and the limb broke, dropping them to the ground.

"Eva, take it easy. I'm still alive, remember?"

"Sorry."

He stood and brushed the seat of his pants. "Why did you say it was too late?"

"Your little stones. They fell."

"What happened?"

"The earthquake."

"What earthquake? I didn't feel anything."

"You were too busy with your books."

"Where's Marcelino, I'll find Marcelino."

"You can't. I said he could go home."

"Why did you do that?"

"He found his alpacas, and he wanted to go home. He said to say goodbye." Evangelina opened her palm. "Here, he left you this."

"What's that?"

"An egg. He said it might bring you luck . . . . He also said we could visit him anytime we wanted."

"Sure, I'll just pretend I have a new pair of lungs. You should see where he lives. You have to be a condor to get there."

"Well, why not?"

"No, I like it here. Have you ever seen such a place? Now this is paradise."

"Lay down, try to rest. We can play when you get up."

"You remember those mojados I brought over?"

Evangelina placed her fingers over his eyes and massaged his temples. "Yes, I remember."

"They're probably here too. I told them it was Tamazunchale,

123

but that sounds like Thomas and Charlie. Maybe I should have called it something else. If they ever learn English, they'll think I was making a joke."

"Nothing wrong with that."

"Eva, can you do the back of my neck. I'm feeling all stiff . . . . There, that's perfect."

"Relax, try to sleep."

"I can't."

"Pretend then. Look at the sky and imagine yourself on a cloud, a nice, soft cloud . . . no noise, not even the sound of your heart, nothing to bother you."

"Eva?"

"Yes."

"Don't go."

"I'm right here, beside you."

"How long do we have?"

"As long as you want."

"Is everybody gone? I don't hear anything."

"No, they're all here."

"All I can hear is the music. You know, I think Marcelino left his music. Would you like to dance?"

"You should be resting."

"Just once . . . ."

The two rose and glided across the park and out over the sea. Carmela waved goodbye, Mario signaled with his thumbs up, and Jess, better late than never, scrambled into the clearing and swore he saw something in the sky.

"A frisbee," Mario said.

"No, it looked like somebody was up there."

"A flying saucer?"

Carmela shaded her eyes. "Don't argue with him, he might change his mind."

"Alright, you saw something."

"Come on, Mario," Carmela said, "let's show him what we can do."

"Wait, I think he's got it. Hey, Jess . . .? Yeah, see, he turned himself into a television."

"Let's go in."

"Okay."

Carmela pulled Mario into the set, and the little girl who found the dead man skipped by and tripped on the cord, snapping the plug from the socket. The girl tickled the knobs, but nothing happened, not even the sound.

Later in the afternoon, when almost everyone had become a shadow, Fausto returned and plugged in the cord. "Just so you'll know I'm still around," he said, then disappeared into the cloud to join his wife. His books, cape, staff, cologne and slippers followed him up. Tico-Tico remained on the ground talking to everyone.

About the only thing Fausto was to regret was his failure to bring cigarettes. He yawned and glanced down one more time. Of all things to forget. I must be getting old. ¡Qué pendejo! And I had two packs under my mattress.

"Fausto?"

"Hmm?"

"Go to sleep."

"It's not perfect . . . you know that, don't you?"

"Lie down and stop talking, you're always talking. And take your slippers off."

Fausto set himself down beside his wife, clapped some life into his cold hands, then crossed them over his chest and went to sleep.

POSTSCRIPT

"TAMAZUNCHALE (Tam-as-un-*cha*-leh, Huastecan, 'Governor's Residence'), former Huastec capital, is a tropical village in Moctezuma River valley on C.N. 85; its sixteenth-century church has been disfigured by recent renovation. A naturalists' and sportsmen's Eden — river fishing from dugouts, mountain game. Moderate hotels are Texas, San Antonio, Quinta Chilla, Mirador.

MOTORIST NOTE: Drive on to Zimapan only during the day to avoid fog when crossing the steep mountain barrier — there is one 5,000-foot climb. Stretches of the road are cut from the solid rock flank of mountains."

—Frances Toor's New Guide to Mexico

Bibliography

Bibliography of Works By and About Ron Arias

Ernestina N. Eger

Ron Arias' writings include both creative literature and journalism. In addition to the works listed here, he wrote during the 1960s for the Copley newspapers and various wire services, with articles appearing in the *New York Times, Christian Science Monitor,* and other publications. Arias' syndicated column series, "Migrants North," was distributed by Hispanic Link (Washington, DC) in 1982 and 1983. This bibliography includes print materials concerning Arias. His works are subdivided by genre and alphabetized by title. Works about Arias, subdivided by type, are alphabetized by author's name. Unseen or unverified items are indicated by an asterisk.

I. Works by Arias

A. Novel and excerpts

1. *The Road to Tamazunchale.* Reno, NV: West Coast Poetry Review, 1975. Tomás Rivera, "Forward" [sic], [p.9].
Rpt. [3rd ed.] 1978.
Rpt. Albuquerque, NM: Pajarito Publications, 1978. José Armas, "Introduction to Pajarito edition," pp. 11–14.
Rpt. Binghamton, NY: Bilingual Press/Editorial Bilingüe, 1986.
2. "Excerpt from *The Road to Tamazunchale.*" *Journal of Ethnic Studies,* 4, 3 (Winter 1976), 61–69.
Rpt. of chapter 3, pp. 22–31.
3. "The Wetback." In *First Chicano Literary Prize, Irvine 1974–1975.* Irvine: Dept. of Spanish and Portuguese, Univ. of California/Irvine, 1975. Pp. 15–23.
Variant of chapter 7, pp. 57–62.

B. Short stories

4. "The Boy Ate Himself." *Quarry West,* No. 13 (1980), pp. 23–27.*
5. "The Castle." *Bilingual Review/Revista Bilingüe,* 3, 2 (May–Aug. 1976), 176–82.
Offprint Jamaica, NY: Bilingual Press/Editorial Bilingüe, 1976.

6. "Chinches." *Latin American Literary Review,* 5, 10 (Spring–Summer 1977), 180–84.

7. "Helping the Poor." *Caracol,* 2, 4 (dic. 1975), 9–11.

8. "A House on the Island (Or, the story of a poetry teacher who seduces her students)." *Revista Chicano-Riqueña,* 3, 4 (otoño 1975), 3–8.

9. "The Interview." *Revista Chicano-Riqueña,* 2, 1 (invierno 1974), 2–6. Rpt. in *Festival de Flor y Canto: An Anthology of Chicano Literature.* Ed. Alurista et al. Los Angeles: Univ. of Southern California Press, 1976. Pp. 7–9.

10. "Lupe." In *Cuentos Chicanos.* Ed. Rudolfo A. Anaya and Antonio Márquez. Special issue of *New America* (Albuquerque, NM), 4, 1 (1980), 55–59.

11. "El Mago." *El Grito,* 3, 3 (Spring 1970), 51–55. Rpt. in *The United States in Literature.* Comp. James E. Miller Jr. et al. Glenview, IL: Scott, Foresman, 1979.*

12. "Perros." *Caracol,* 2, 5 (enero 1976), 6–7.

13. "Stoop Labor." *Revista Chicano-Riqueña,* 2, 1 (invierno 1974), 7–14.

14. "The Story Machine." *Revista Chicano-Riqueña,* 3, 4 (otoño 1975), 9–12.

C. Play

15. "The Interview." *Revista Chicano-Riqueña,* 7, 1 (invierno 1979), 1–7. Adaptation of item 8.

D. Essays, journalism, and reviews

16. "Accent: Margarita Inventor." *Nuestro,* 2, 8 (Aug. 1978), 44–45.

17. "After Eight Hours of Arduous Labor, Rescue Ace Frederic Pierre Plucks a Miracle From the Quake Ruins." *People,* 23, 16 (14 October 1985), 157–59.

18. "Argentines and Falklanders." *Los Angeles Times,* 12 April 1982, Sec. II, p. 7.

19. "The Barrio." *IUD Agenda* (AFL/CIO, Washington, DC), July 1966, pp. 15–17. Rpt. in *The Chicanos: Mexican American Voices.* Ed. Ed Ludwig and James Santibáñez. Baltimore, MD: Penguin Books, 1971. Pp. 123–26.

20. "The Best Kept Secret of the Latino Entertainment World." *Nuestro,* 2, 11 (Nov. 1978), 49–50. About Chuy Negrete.

21. "A Better Approach to Mental Health." *Nuestro,* 2, 10 (Oct. 1978), 28.

22. "A Black-Latino Coalition." *Los Angeles Times,* 23 Sept. 1980, Sec. II.

23. Review of *Bless Me, Ultima,* by Rudolfo A. Anaya. *American Book Review,* 1, 6 (March-April 1979), 8.

24. "Chicano Books a Rare Item." *El Chicano* (San Bernardino, CA), 5, 26 (17 Nov. 1971), pp. 3, 10.

25. "Chicano Literature for English Classes." *Inside English* (CA Junior College English Teachers), Spring 1975.*

26. "Children of the Barrio: We're Supposed to Believe We're Inferior." *IUD Agenda* (AFL/CIO, Washington, DC), July 1966, pp. 18–20.

Rpt. in *The Chicanos: Mexican American Voices.* Ed. Ed Ludwig and James Santibáñez. Baltimore, MD: Penguin Books, 1971. Pp. 173–76.

27. Review of *Contemporary Chicano Theatre,* ed Roberto J. Garza. *Journal of Ethnic Studies,* 5, 1 (Spring 1977), 122–23.

28. "The Distortion of Cinco de Mayo." *Los Angeles Times,* 4 May 1979, Sec. II, p. 7.

29. "The Doctor Who Might Have Been Bumped by Bakke." *Nuestro,* 2, 2 (Feb. 1978), 22–24.
About James Méndez and Henry Gonzales.

30. "Getting on the Set." *Nuestro,* 1, 7 (Oct. 1977), 18–21.
About Latino representation in the TV and film industry.

31. "In Search of El Dorado." *Atlanta Journal and Constitution,* 4 Dec. 1983, "Atlanta Weekly Magazine," pp. 28–32.*

32. "Looking Back." *Nuestro,* 3, 10 (Nov. 1979), 60.
Record review of *Rise,* by Herb Alpert, and *The Chicano Experience.*

33. "Making the Snakes Cry with Envy." *Nuestro,* 1, 6 (Sept. 1977), 24–25.
About lowriders.

34. "Marcial Ayala." *Southwestern Art,* 7, 1 (Fall 1978).*

35. "The Mexican Way of Death." *Los Angeles Times,* 2 Nov. 1981, Sec. II.*

36. "Nurses Have Come a Long Way, Baby." *Nuestro,* 2, 12 (Dec. 1978), 14–16.

37. "The Problem That Won't Go Away: Marielitos." *Atlanta Journal and Constitution,* 1 Jan. 1984, "Atlanta Weekly Magazine," p. 14.*

38. "The Quiet Revolution." *Nuestro,* 1, 5 (Aug. 1977), 7–8.
About California politics.

39. "Red Wine, Hemingway and Me." *People,* 23, 16 (14 October 1985), 154.

40. "Regional Report: Health." *Nuestro,* 3, 1 (Jan.–Feb. 1979), 13.

41. "The Rooster That Called Me Home." *Nation,* 236, 24 (18 June 1983), 758–61.
Rpt. as "Roosters and Saints." In *While Someone Else Is Eating.* Ed. Earl Shorris with Eric Etheridge and Sylvia Sasson. Garden City, NY: Doubleday/Anchor, 1984. Pp. 77–86.

42. "*Santo* of the Synagogue." *Nuestro,* 2, 6 (June 1978), pp. 16, 55.
About José Cruz Burciaga.

43. "El señor del chivo." *Journal of Ethnic Studies,* 3, 4 (Winter 1976), 58–60.

44. "Sick to Death of the Health Mess." *Nuestro,* 2, 10 (Oct. 1978), pp. 24–25, 29–30.

45. "Sorrow and Strength Amid the Ruins." *People,* 23, 15 (7 October 1985), 137–38, 145, 147.
About Mexico City earthquake.

46. Review of *Zoot-Suit Murders,* by Thomas Sánchez. *American Book Review,* 2, 1 (Summer 1979), 9.

II. Works about Arias

E. Critical articles and papers

47. Bruce-Novoa. "The Expanding Space of Chicano Literature. Update: 1978." Paper presented at Canto al Pueblo, Corpus Christi, TX, 5 June 1978.

48. Cárdenas de Dwyer, Carlota. "International Literary Metaphor and Ron Arias: An Analysis of *The Road to Tamazunchale.*" *Bilingual Review/Revista Bilingüe,* 4, 3 (Sept.–Dec. 1977), 229–33.

Rpt. in *The Identification and Analysis of Chicano Literature.* Ed. Francisco Jiménez. New York: Bilingual Press/Editorial Bilingüe, 1979. Pp. 358–64. Paper presented at Canto al Pueblo, Corpus Christi, TX, 5 June 1978.

49. Gingerich, Willard. "Arias, Ronald Francis." In *Chicano Literature: A Reference Guide.* Ed. Julio A. Martínez and Francisco A. Lomelí. Westport, CT: Greenwood Press, 1985. Pp. 51–64.

50. Lattin, Vernon E. "Art and Reality in *The Road to Tamazunchale.*" Paper presented at Mountain Interstate Foreign Language Conference, Oct. 1978.

51. ———. "The 'Creation of Death' in Ron Arias' *The Road to Tamazunchale.*" *Revista Chicano-Riqueña,* 10, 3 (Summer 1982), 53–62.

52. ———. "The Quest for Mythic Vision in Contemporary Native American and Chicano Fiction." *American Literature,* 50, 4 (Jan. 1979), 625–40.

53. Lewis, Marvin A. *Introduction to the Chicano Novel.* Institute Paper Series. Milwaukee: Univ. of Wisconsin/Milwaukee, College of Letters and Science, Spanish Speaking Outreach Institute, 1982. Pp. 49–52 et passim.

54. ———. "On *The Road to Tamazunchale.*" *Revista Chicano-Riqueña,* 5, 4 (otoño 1977), 49–52.

55. ———. "The Urban Experience in Selected Chicano Fiction." *Selected Proceedings of the 4th Annual Conference on Minority Studies,* Vol. 6, "Minority Literature and the Urban Experience." April 1976. Ed. George E. Carter and James R. Parker. La Crosse, WI: Institute for Minority Studies, Univ. of Wisconsin, 1978. Pp. 85–94.

Rpt. in *Contemporary Chicano Fiction: A Critical Survey.* Ed. Vernon E. Lattin. Binghamton, NY: Bilingual Press/Editorial Bilingüe, 1986. Pp. 46–61.

56. Marín, Mariana. "*The Road to Tamazunchale:* Fantasy or Reality?" *De Colores,* 3, 4 [1977], 34–38.

57. Martínez, Eliud. "Ron Arias' *The Road to Tamazunchale:* A Chicano Novel of the New Reality." *Latin American Literary Review,* 5, 10 (Spring–Summer 1977), 51–63.

Rpt. in *Contemporary Chicano Fiction: A Critical Survey.* Ed. Vernon E. Lattin. Binghamton, NY: Bilingual Press/Editorial Bilingüe, 1986. Pp. 226–38.

58. Nieto, Eva Margarita. "The Dialectics of Textual Interpolation in Ron Arias' *The Road to Tamazunchale.*" In *Contemporary Chicano Fiction: A Critical Survey.* Ed. Vernon E. Lattin. Binghamton, NY: Bilingual Press/Editorial Bilingüe, 1986. Pp. 239–46.

59. Rabinowitz, Sima. "A Study in Apocalyptic Visions." Paper presented at Popular Culture Assn., Pittsburgh, 26 April 1979.

60. Robinson, Cecil. *Mexico and the Hispanic Southwest in American Literature.* Tucson: Univ. of Arizona, 1977. Pp. 330-31.

61. Saldívar, Ramón. "A Dialectic of Difference: Towards a Theory of the Chicano Novel." *MELUS,* 6, 3 (Fall 1979), 73-92. Rpt. in *Contemporary Chicano Fiction: A Critical Survey.* Ed. Vernon E. Lattin. Binghamton, NY: Bilingual Press/Editorial Bilingüe, 1986. Pp. 13-31.

62. Tatum, Charles M. *Chicano Literature.* TUSAS 433. Boston: Twayne Publishers, 1982. Pp. 100-01, 128-31 et passim.

F. Theses and dissertations

63. Saldívar, José David. "Claiming the Americas: Contemporary Third World Literature." *DAI,* 43, 11 (May 1983), 3589A.

64. Vallejos, Thomas. "Mestizaje: The Transformations of Ancient Indian Religious Thought in Contemporary Chicano Fiction." *DAI,* 41, 4 (Oct. 1980), 1602A.

G. Reviews and bibliographic annotations

65. Bonazzi, Robert. Review of *The Road to Tamazunchale. Library Journal,* 101, 3 (1 Feb. 1976), 546.

66. Cano, Gabriel. "Letras chicanas." *Plural,* No. 62 (Nov. 1976), p. 84.

67. Cheuse, Alan. "Death of Chicano Everyman." *Los Angeles Times,* 7 Dec. 1975, "Book Review," p. 4.

68. Firman, C. K. "Realism, Fantasy Combined in Novel." *Progress-Bulletin* (Pomona, CA), 2 Nov. 1975, p. 30.*

69. Gingerich, Willard. "Chicanismo: The Rebirth of a Spirit." *Southwest Review,* 62, 3 (Summer 1977), pp. vi-vii, 302-04.

70. Islas, Arturo. "Magic Realism in East Los Angeles." To be published in *New Mexico Sun.*

71. Lomelí, Francisco A., and Donaldo W. Urioste. *Chicano Perspectives in Literature: A Critical and Annotated Bibliography.* Albuquerque, NM: Pajarito Publications, 1976. Pp. 41-42, 66, 92, 98, 103, 105.

72. Review of *The Road to Tamazunchale. Sipapu* (Winters, CA), 7, 1 (Jan. 1976), 22.

73. Rodríguez, Juan. Comments on *The Road to Tamazunchale. Carta Abierta,* No. 1 (28 Oct. 1975), p. 1.

74. ———. Comments on *The Road to Tamazunchale. Carta Abierta,* No. 2 [Nov.-Dec. 1975], p. 1.

75. Rothfork, John. Review of *The Road to Tamazunchale. New Mexico Humanities Review,* 3, 1 (1980), 73.*

76. Salinas, Judy. Review of *The Road to Tamazunchale. Latin American Literary Review,* 4, 8 (Spring-Summer 1976), 111-12.

77. Tatum, Charles M. *A Selected and Annotated Bibliography of Chicano Studies.* [Manhattan, KS: Kansas State Univ.,] Society of Spanish and Spanish American Studies, 1976. Item 255.

133

Ernestina N. Eger

Second edition. Lincoln, NE: Univ. of Nebraska, SSSAS, Modern Languages and Literatures, 1979. Items 405, 409, 415, 416, 423, 445.
78. Vigil, Evangelina. "Critical Review: *The Road to Tamazunchale*, a novel by Ron Arias." To be published in *Synergy* (Houston, TX).
79. Zamora, Bernice. Review of *The Road to Tamazunchale*. Atisbos, [No. 3] Summer–Fall 1978, pp. 226–28.
80. Zimmerman, Enid. "An Annotated Bibliography of Chicano Literature: Novels, Short Fiction, Poetry, and Drama, 1970–1980." *Bilingual Review/Revista Bilingüe*, 9, 3 (Sept.–Dec. 1982), 232.

H. Interviews

81. Bruce-Novoa, [Juan]. "Interview with Ron Arias." *Journal of Ethnic Studies*, 3, 4 (Winter 1976), 70–73.
Revised and amplified version in *Chicano Authors: Inquiry by Interview*. Austin & London: Univ. of Texas Press, 1980. Pp. 235–52.
82. "Para la comunidad, los intelectuales 'de la raza' somos vistos como unos bichos raros, dice Ron Arias." *Uno más uno* (México, DF), 11 junio 1980, p. 16.
83. Rodríguez del Pino, Salvador. "La novela chicana de los setenta comentada por sus escritores y críticos." *Bilingual Review/Revista Bilingüe*, 4, 3 (Sept.–Dec. 1977), 240–44.
Rpt. in *The Identification and Analysis of Chicano Literature*. Ed. Francisco Jiménez. New York: Bilingual Press/Editorial Bilingüe, 1979. Pp. 153–60.

I. Biographical listing and news articles

84. Acker, John. "Chicano Authors at UCLA." *La Gente* (UCLA), 11, 4 (March 1981), 3.
85. Martínez, Julio A., ed. *Chicano Scholars and Writers: A Bio-Bibliographical Directory*. Metuchen, NJ, & London: Scarecrow Press, 1979. Pp. 28–29.
86. Valadez, Kathy L. "Chicano wins literary award." *El Chicano* (San Bernardino, CA), 9, 10 (9 Aug. 1973), 3.

CARTHAGE COLLEGE